Praise f

“As graceful and cont
ing.”

—NPR Books

“Wise readers will hop on this train now, as the journey promises to be breathtaking.”

—Robin Hobb, author of The Assassin’s Apprentice

“This is an impressive performance.”

—*Publishers Weekly*

“I am impressed… An exceedingly inventive story in a lushly realized dark setting that is not your uncle’s Medieval Europe. I’ll be looking forward to the next installment.”

—Glen Cook, author of *The Black Company*

“Bradley P. Beaulieu’s new fantasy epic is filled with memorable characters, enticing mysteries, and a world so rich in sensory detail that you can feel the desert breeze in your hair as you read. Çeda is hands-down one of the best heroines in the genre—strong, resourceful, and fiercely loyal to friends and family. Fantasy doesn’t get better than this!”

—C. S. Friedman, author of the Coldfire and Magister trilogies

“Exotic, sumptuous and incredibly entertaining, Beaulieu has created memorable characters in a richly imagined world.”

—Michael J. Sullivan, author of *The Riyria Chronicles*

“Beaulieu’s intricate world-building and complex characters are quickly becoming the hallmarks of his writing, and if this opening volume is any indication, The Song of the Shattered Sands promises to be one of the next great fantasy epics.”

—Jim Kellen, Science Fiction and Fantasy Book Buyer for Barnes & Noble

“Beaulieu’s fantasy worlds are well-imagined and richly drawn…the kind you want to keep visiting.”

—Kirkus Speculative Reading List for September 2015

Also by Bradley P. Beaulieu

The Song of the Shattered Sands

Of Sand and Malice Made
Twelve Kings in Sharakhai
With Blood Upon the Sand
A Veil of Spears

Shattered Sands Novellas

The Doors at Dusk and Dawn
In the Village Where Brightwine Flows
The Tattered Prince and the Demon Veiled
A Wasteland of My God's Own Making

The Lays of Anuskaya

The Winds of Khalakovo
The Straits of Galahesh
The Flames of Shadam Khoreh

Short Story Collections

Lest Our Passage Be Forgotten & Other Stories
In the Stars I'll Find You & Other Tales of Futures Fantastic

Novellas

The Burning Light (with Rob Zeigler)
Strata (with Stephen Gaskell)

The Doors at Dusk and Dawn

Bradley Beaulieu

Cover art by René Aigner © 2017
Cover design by Bradley P. Beaulieu
Author photo courtesy of Al Bogdan

First Edition: October 2017

ISBN: 978-1-93964-926-3 (Paperback)
ISBN: 978-1-93964-924-9 (epub)
ISBN: 978-1-93964-925-6 (Kindle)

Please visit me on the web at
http://www.quillings.com

THE DOORS AT DUSK AND DAWN

The desert was bright and the wind was gusting when the ships of Tribe Rafik took in their sails. Ships of various builds and sizes came to rest in an orderly arc, nearly three dozen in all, their dark hulls sitting in stark contrast to the swaths of open desert beyond. On the decks and around the ships, hundreds of Rafik women, children, and men began to unload tents, supplies, food, firewood, even horses, along the gangplanks, all in anticipation of the coming competition and the days of celebration that both preceded and followed.

All too soon, Devorah, a young woman of eighteen summers, was holding an iron tent stake in place while her twin sister, Leorah, used a heavy wooden mallet to drive it into the sand. Over and over the mallet struck home, Leorah's well muscled arms driving it much faster, much *harder*, than Devorah ever could. She seemed almost angered by it, as if, after being trapped in a ship for so long, she wished to work out all her pent-up energy on the very first stake.

"Careful," Devorah said. "You'll knock yourself out like Old Khyrn did the other day."

With one final grunt and a full-bodied swing, Leorah brought the mallet down. Then she arched her back and wiped her brow, breathing heavy as a wisp of her long, dark bangs slipped loose from the autumn-colored scarf tied around her head. Her copper skin shone with sweat, making the blue crescent moon tattoos over her temples stand out. "Old Khyrn knocked himself out whittling one time," she said between breaths. "I'll be fine."

While Devorah set the next spike, Leorah stuffed the lock of hair back beneath her scarf and hoisted the mallet back up to her shoulder. Then she set to—*thump, thump, thump*—while all around, dozens of others from Tribe Rafik busied themselves pitching tents of their own.

"Who's this now?" Devorah asked, catching movement along the horizon.

It was a sandship, and it was heading straight for their encampment. A great tail of dust billowed behind the ship like an amber ostrich plume caught in a breeze. Beyond it, the Great Shangazi's western mountains curved in a grand arc.

A ship of Kundhun? Devorah mused. *Or perhaps Qaimir?*

Few of the desert tribes sailed galleons. They were often too big. Too slow. Indeed, its silhouette was bulky and ponderous; it tilted awkwardly to port or starboard as it navigated the lazy dunes. Still, its stout skimwood skis, its three tall masts, and its set of billowing sails seemed to be carrying it over the sands well enough.

Leorah shaded her eyes and stared out across the sand. Her face soured the longer she looked. "That's a royal galleon."

Devorah peered more carefully at the ship, then saw it: the highest pennant bore the sign of the Sharakhani Kings, a shield with twelve shamshirs fanned around it. "A royal galleon…" Devorah spit onto the sand. "Why would they have come?"

"They've come to partake in the traverse," came a voice behind them.

Devorah and Leorah turned to find Armesh walking toward them. He wore not a turban, as most in the tribe did, but a simple agal and ghutrah. He was a man of forty summers with a long, wiry beard and kindly eyes that matched his soft manners. He was the husband to Şelal Ymine'ala al Rafik, the tribe's charismatic shaikh, but Devorah and Leorah knew him as the man who'd done the most to shelter them after their parents and younger brother had been killed four years earlier. Armesh had known their mother and father. Known them quite well, in fact. They'd been raised together in the northern reaches of the desert in Tribe Tulogal, decades before Armesh had found himself married off to Şelal.

The traverse Armesh had referred to was a legendary horse race more formally known as Annam's Traverse. It was held once every three years in this very place, a competition attended by three tribes, who each put forth champions in hopes of taking the top prize.

As Armesh neared, Leorah set the mallet down and pulled herself up. The two of them were of a height, but Leorah's more muscled frame made her seem taller. "Why would the Kings wish to take part in a *traverse*?"

Armesh shrugged, an innocent gesture from a man who surely knew more than he was letting on. "Perhaps they merely wish to test their mettle, as the rest of the tribes do."

"More likely they've come hoping to steal our glory before rubbing our noses in it." Leorah had said it under her breath but still loudly enough for Armesh to hear. "It's what they're best at, no?"

Armesh's reply was even more muted. "You would do well to keep such thoughts to yourself, Leorah. Speak no ill of the Kings." He spread his arms wide, a gesture that encompassed the entirety of the burgeoning camp around them. "It would reflect poorly not only on you, but the whole of the tribe."

"Of course," Devorah said, stepping in before Leorah could say something foolish. "We're grateful for our place here. You know this."

"*I* do"—Armesh's pleasant smile returned—"but many of the others still do not, so you'll watch your tongue, won't you?" He stared fixedly at Leorah as he strode away, making for the center of the camp. He joined his wife, Şelal, who was speaking with the tribe's elders, several of whom eyed the approaching galleon with guarded expressions.

With Leorah still staring at Armesh's back, working her jaw back and forth, Devorah picked up another stake. "No time for dawdling," she said, snapping her fingers. "We have work to do."

Leorah stared at the mallet, still held loosely in her right hand. "Careful who you're snapping those fingers at." She lifted the mallet high. "You're speaking to a woman who holds your fate in her hands."

Down the mallet came, but it was uncharacteristically off target, and the head skipped off, narrowly missing Leorah's hands.

"Ho!" Devorah shouted. "My turn!" And took the mallet away.

Smiling, Leorah knelt and held the stake. "So easy to manipulate…"

"How little you know. I *wanted* the mallet all along." She swung, and the mallet came down with a pathetic smack.

Staring at it for a moment, both of them burst into laughter.

Over the next few hours, the camp filled in around them. Men and women moved along the lengthening aisles like boats on a river. Tents and pavilions dominated once open spaces. Large piles of firewood were laid out near the cooking pits and in the large space to the north of camp, a circle of celebration where all three attending tribes would gather and sing songs, trade tales and drink spirits. It was one of the largest gatherings the desert knew. Tribes Rafik, Okan, and

Narazid would all come in hopes of putting forth a champion who could win the traverse. But even if they didn't, it was a time to renew ties with their sister tribes.

When they finished with their own tent and helped erect several others near them, Devorah and Leorah helped with the food. The air was laced with lemon and rosemary and the smell of roasting goat. Children ran shouting and playing while their elders bellowed for them to behave. Who could blame the children, though? They'd been cooped up in the ships for the past two weeks as they'd journeyed toward the site of the traverse.

Over the course of the day, other ships sailed in. A dozen flying the black-wing banners of Okan came near midday. A bare handful from Narazid arrived shortly before nightfall. The royal galleon anchored some half-league distant, but no one came forth to greet Şelal or anyone else. Şelal was forced to send Armesh to greet *them* and welcome them to the western reaches of the Great Shangazi.

"Bloody cowards," Leorah said as they approached Bagra, the tribe's physic, ready to help carry her things into her tent.

"Stop it," Devorah said while shooting a glance toward Bagra. A notorious night owl, she was nodding off in her folding chair by the entrance. Every so often she'd snort, shake herself awake and look around wildly, then rest her hands over her soft belly once more. "There's nothing to be gained by poking the Kings of Sharakhai with a sharp stick."

Inside the tent, Leorah threw down the carpet she had slung over her shoulder. "Don't you start, too."

Devorah kicked the carpet so that it rolled out, then set Bagra's musty bedding atop it. She gripped Leorah's shoulders and spoke softly but forcefully. "The wounds are still fresh for me too. I still wake thinking they're sleeping across the tent from us. I wish there was something we could do, but we can't. They're dead. We nearly were too. But by the grace of the gods, we've found ourselves in a new tribe with people willing to shelter us."

Leorah sneered. "By the grace of the gods…"

Devorah held up her forefinger, an echo of their father when he was mad. "I *mean* it. Enough. Set the past aside. The traverse is about to begin. Just think how grand it will be seeing the Kings lose to us!"

At last, a hint of a smile showed on Leorah's full lips. "It *will* be grand, won't it?"

That night, food was shared between the Biting Shields of Tribe Rafik, the Black Wings of Tribe Okan, and the few Bloody Manes of Tribe Narazid who'd arrived. No one from the Kings' galleon came, though many had exited the ship. They'd set up a small camp beyond it, but not a single one had approached to share in the tribes' fires. Some wondered why they would travel so far and not at least break bread with the desert folk, but none shed a tear; the Kings were tolerated in the desert, little more.

The following day, dozens more ships arrived. Horses were carried on many of them, tall beasts with glittering coats of iron and copper and brass and gold. These were the akhalas, the giants of the desert, horses that pastured in the mountains while the tribes sailed the sands of the Great Shangazi on their fleets of sandships. During the warmer months the tribes returned and used them for hunting and sport and the simple joy of ranging the world on such magnificent beasts. The akhalas of Tribe Narazid sported bright red manes, dusted as they were in sanguine chalk. It made them look feral and crazed as they sprinted over the sand or over the hard earth near the mountains. Those of Tribe Rafik and Okan were just as grand, bedecked with glittering bridles, rich leather saddles, and bright blankets with cloth tassels.

Near the Kings' ship, a lone man rode tirelessly over

the desert. He split his time between three different horses, perhaps those he'd trained simultaneously in case one turned up lame. Now and again he came near the edge of the Tribes' camp, but he never entered it, nor spoke to anyone, as if he'd been ordered not to or thought himself above it. Leorah was incensed by him, but Devorah, though she'd never admit it to Leorah, was intrigued. He was tall and, from what little she could tell over such a distance, quite handsome. His long black hair flowed freely behind him, not so differently from his favored horse, an akhala with a lustrous onyx tail. By the gods, he looked as if he'd been *born* on the silver beast.

"Bloody gods," Leorah said, "why don't you just spread your legs on the sand before him and have done?" She was stitching an amberlark along the hem of a dress she'd been embellishing over the past week. She'd noticed Devorah's wandering eyes, perhaps more often than Devorah had realized.

Devorah returned to her painting of a clay water ewer. She *had* been watching the rider, and for decidedly longer than was proper. Still, without even really willing it, she kept looking whenever Leorah's back was turned.

That night, the first official feast of the traverse

was held. All three tribes were present. And this time, the Kings' contingent did come. There were a dozen in attendance—the bent form of King Sukru foremost among them. He was a wizened man with small eyes and a hard stare. He seemed to take everything in around him with a covetous look, as if he considered the desert his own possession and wondered at the gall of the tribes who'd dared step foot in it. Devorah noted the whip coiled at his side—a weapon, it was said, given to him by the god of war, Thaash himself.

When Sukru was offered food and wine, he seemed to relax. He ate, as did the others, men and women from Sharakhai, the desert's Amber Jewel, who were of no tribe and all tribes at the same time. To Devorah's great interest, the lone rider came as well. His name was Kirhan, and he was as handsome as he'd seemed from a distance. Once or twice, to her horror, he caught her staring at him. And to her great annoyance, she also caught his eye wandering toward Leorah. Leorah was the loudest. She joked the most. She flirted. She was the one who got the looks—from men, from women, it didn't matter. Devorah wasn't like her. Never had been. She was the quiet one, the moon to Leorah's sun.

Kirhan spoke for a long while with Şelal. Devorah somehow managed to take her eyes off him—long enough to finish her bowl of honeyed rice and lamb, in any case. She felt certain he'd already forgotten about her, but when she looked over at him again, he was staring straight at her.

He laughed as she quickly turned away.

Sand and stone, how she hoped the fire's ruddy light was enough to hide the flush in her cheeks.

After the meal ended, a space was cleared. Şelal stepped into it and filled it with her presence. She was a fit woman of nearly fifty summers. The black in her hair was slowly giving way to grey, but that only seemed to intensify her steely gaze, the sharp way in which she spoke. It even made her bearing, that of a statue crafted from granite, seem even more godlike than it already did.

"Three years have passed since we last met," she began. "As we have for centuries, we come once again to rejoice. We come to share tales of the desert. We come to meet those new to each tribe and to lament those no longer with us." An eerie chorus of whistles lifted up in honor of the dead. It sent a chill down Devorah's spine for her lost mother and father, for her little brother, all of whom were lost before the last traverse.

An outsider might think the whistles were meant for Devorah's lost family. They were not. They were for the twelve tribes of the desert, not the thirteenth, the lost tribe to which Devorah and Leorah both properly belonged. It was why the two of them had fled and begged for a place in Tribe Rafik. The attack that had killed their parents had been a complete surprise, an ambush during a terrible sandstorm. Word came that the Kings' soldiers, the Silver Spears, had been involved. How the Kings had learned of them she had no idea, but the explanation was likely simple enough. Was the desert not full of tales of men, women, even children, taking up the Kings' bounty to identify members of the thirteenth tribe?

Whatever the reason, one thing was clear: the only way to remain alive had been to flee. For years their mother and father had been drilling it into them. It was why they'd come to Armesh; as the shaikh's husband, he held high status in Tribe Rafik, and he'd used it to secure their place in the tribe. Even so, they'd been forced to bargain away nearly everything of value to ensure their heritage remained secret.

"We have also come for Annam's Traverse," Şelal continued, "a race that begins with the coming dawn and runs until a lone champion has been declared victorious."

A joyous roar filled the night. The men stomped

their feet. The women ululated their high calls, "Lai, lai, lai!" The youngest, babes and skirt-holders, watched with wide-eyed fascination, some with outright fear, others with so much unbridled joy they burst out laughing at the carnival of sights and sounds around them.

Şelal took all this in with a satisfied air, a performer in that moment as much as a leader. "Tomorrow, the first contest begins, a race of endurance, one that will last many days and cross many leagues over the desert. It is but the first of the challenges that await our champions. The first ten to return will enter the second contest"—she pointed west, where the outline of an imposing mountain could be seen, dark and brooding beneath a scintillant sky—"a climb to the very pinnacle of Annam's Crook, a peak that challenges even the finest horses, the most skilled climbers. The first two to return from that dread peak will be entered into the third and final contest, mounted combat in which the winner need but knock their opponent from their horse in any way they can.

"Those who compete," Şelal continued amid cheers, "will gain the undying respect of all three tribes." She waved to King Sukru. "As well as that of our visiting King."

At this, the cheers settled considerably. Not completely so—the tribes were not so foolish that they would risk insulting a King of Sharakhai to his face—but it was a clear sleight. Sukru, for his part, hadn't seemed to pay attention. He was staring at Şelal with an expression of boredom, as if the concerns of the desert and its tribes were of no more importance than the ever-changing shape of the dunes.

Şelal went on quickly, somehow managing to appear unhurried as she did so. "There is more!" She spread her arms as if to encompass the sky. "Much more. Each of our tribes, and King Sukru, have brought a prize!" She waved toward Sukru first, who flicked one hand absently to a stately woman by his side. The woman, Sukru's vizira, if rumors were true, opened a small chest. In the chest were stacks and stacks of golden rahl—coins stamped with the mark of the Kings. It was a symbol of Sharakhai's power, and so, a symbol of oppression in the desert, but no tribe would scoff at such a prize. It would do much to help them through tough winters, or better prepare them for skirmishes with the tribes of Kundhun, which had become all too frequent of late.

Şelal bowed to King Sukru. "From the Kings, a chest of gold awaits the winner of Annam's Traverse!"

Şelal then waved to Duyal, the shaikh of Tribe Okan, a burly man in a pure white thawb and ivory turban who held a finely crafted shamshir with an etched blade. The metal was dark. Not so dark as the ebon steel of Sharakhai's famed Blade Maidens, but enough to make it clear that the blade itself was of extremely high quality. "From the Black Wings, the Sword of the Willow awaits!"

Next she addressed the shaikh of Tribe Narazid, a tall oak of a man named Jherrok who lifted high above his head a golden chalice, bejeweled with rubies and emeralds. "From the Bloody Manes, the golden chalice of Bahri Al'sir awaits!"

Here Şelal paused, building the anticipation. "And from the Biting Shields!" She spun in a circle, arms raised, a gesture both formal and inviting. Then, with a flourish, she lowered her left hand and lifted her right high overhead.

Despite herself, Devorah gasped. She wasn't sure when Şelal had done it, but a ring now adorned her forefinger. It had a beautiful setting, but it was the jewel that attracted the eye. It was a massive amethyst that glinted brightly in the firelight.

Before Şelal could say more, someone behind Devorah uttered a single word in a long, terrible scream. *"No!"*

Devorah turned in time to see Leorah stalking forward. Devorah immediately intercepted her, and when Leorah tried to stalk past, she stopped her with both hands to her chest.

"You cannot have it!" Leorah shouted at Şelal.

"Leorah, *stop it,*" Devorah hissed.

But Leorah didn't care. Her eyes, her anger, were only for Şelal. *"You cannot have it!"*

Şelal stared evenly, almost amusedly, at the spectacle unfolding before her. All around, the tribe watched in silence. Many were shocked or confused. Only a handful were aware the ring even existed, and likely only Şelal and Armesh knew it had once belonged to Devorah and Leorah's mother. Most, however, knew that they'd come to Tribe Rafik under strange circumstances, which was why the anger in some people's eyes worried Devorah so. The King might wonder after the story behind this ring. He might ask questions of Şelal. How long would it take for him to wonder if they were from the lost tribe? The conclusion might not be a simple one to reach, but neither was it all that difficult. And if Sukru *did* reach it, or even suspect it might be true, their fates would be sealed.

As Sukru eyed them with something like amusement, Devorah gripped Leorah's arms tightly. "Leorah, don't do this," she whispered harshly. "For once, control your temper."

Leorah was breathing heavily. Her eyes were afire as they fixed on the amethyst ring still raised high on Şelal's right hand. She looked as if she knew she was about to make a terrible mistake, but no longer cared.

"Do you have anything to say, Leorah?" Şelal asked with a calm that was beginning to light a fire in Devorah's heart as well.

Devorah whispered into Leorah's ear before she could say another word, "You seal *both* our fates with your next words."

At last, the fury in Leorah's heart seemed to cool. With the release of one deep breath, her body lost much of its pent-up tension. "No, my shaikh."

Devorah immediately guided her away, leading her into the darkness as the sand grasped at their sandals. Behind, the celebration resumed, the entire crowd raising their voices in excitement over the prospect of winning the spoils of the traverse, or having someone in their tribe declared victor.

"Leorah," Devorah said, spinning her around, "you've got to control your *temper*."

Leorah stabbed her finger over Devorah's shoulder,

toward the sound of celebration. "That is our *mother's* ring. That is *her* gemstone. Our birthright."

"I know very well what it is."

"She has no right to offer it up as a prize! She *promised* us we could work to win it back."

"She's apparently changed her mind. You know very well we'd likely ceded it to her when we found our place here."

"We do our work. We pull our own weight."

"I know," Devorah said, "and we are alive because of it. It was ours once, Leorah, but no longer. Let it go. It is a *thing*. We still have each other, and I would not lose *you* because you couldn't stand the thought of giving it up."

For the first time, Leorah seemed to *see* Devorah. Truly see her. Whatever words she'd been about to say withered on the vine, and Leorah took her in anew. "I don't know what I'd do without you," she said, and took Devorah into a deep embrace.

"Likely die while raging at the desert for being too hot."

"It *is* too hot."

"So are you."

Leorah laughed, and Devorah laughed with her.

When Devorah woke in their tent the next morning, Leorah was gone. She made some flatbread on their small oven, hoping she'd return. When she didn't, Devorah searched the camp, but saw no sign of her, nor, apparently, had anyone else. It made Devorah instantly nervous, as if Leorah were planning something rash. Şelal had overlooked Leorah's outburst during the feast, but she wouldn't do so again.

Devorah made her way, slowly at first, then at a tilting run, toward the center of the camp. *Please don't make a fool of me, Leorah.* At the entrance to the largest of Tribe Rafik's tents, she found Şelal lounging with Armesh, both sipping tea on the long square carpet beneath the sunshade.

"Ah," Şelal said easily as she plucked a fat red grape from the nearby table. "If it isn't our wayward daughter."

"Good morning, Şelal," Devorah said. "Armesh."

"I'm surprised I didn't see you last night." She spoke with a forced ease, her anger thinly veiled.

"Begging your forgiveness, we only thought to leave you to the festivities. Unhindered, as it were. I hope you can find it in your heart to pardon our outburst."

"*Our* outburst?" She popped the grape into her mouth and munched on it loudly. "It seems to me *you* can hardly be blamed for *Leorah's* outburst."

"She was caught off-guard. We both were. We'd thought…"

"Thought what?"

"We'd thought the stone still ours."

"Yours? After sailing my ships for nearly four years? After eating my bread, drinking my wine?"

"You'd said we could work off the cost…"

"And you think you've done enough to gain *this* back?"

Her right hand had been hidden behind the armrest of her low wooden chair, but now Devorah could see that she was still wearing the ring. Şelal examined it with leisure. It was a show, of course, a way for Şelal to prove that she and she alone ruled this tribe. It was also meant to make Devorah feel small and helpless. And it was working.

"With the speed at which you two work," Şelal said, "this ring would take a lifetime to earn back. Even then, I fear you would still owe me a chest of rahl like the one Sukru showed us last night."

"You said we need but work faithfully, diligently,

and the ring would be returned to us."

"Well, you weren't exactly honest about the nature of the ring, were you?"

"What do you mean?"

Armesh was staring into his teacup, avoiding Devorah's gaze.

"Come, come. Surely you're aware of its properties?"

Devorah could only shake her head. The gods of the desert as her witnesses, she had no idea what Şelal was talking about. Her mother had never mentioned anything about it, and Devorah herself had hardly worn it before it was gone, taken by Şelal as the price of entry into the tribe.

Şelal pushed herself up off the chair, smoothed the wrinkles from the front of her blue jalabiya. "Well, if you're not aware, then it hardly seems appropriate for *me* to tell you, does it?"

She strolled toward the center of the camp, leaving a terrible chill in her wake. Devorah had always felt small and weak in this tribe, but she'd never felt like chattel. Not until now. Something had changed, and the only thing Devorah could point to was Sukru.

She turned to Armesh, who looked as uncomfortable as Devorah ever remembered seeing him. "What does the ring do, Armesh?"

He stared intently at the tea in his cup as he swirled it around. He downed the last of it, then stood, looking suddenly and uncharacteristically resolute. "There's much to do before the race begins, Devorah." He turned and headed toward the door of his tent. "Best you go and help."

Devorah grabbed his arm and spun him around. "Why does Sukru want the amethyst?"

The determination in Armesh's eyes transformed into a boiling rage. "You would do well to release me, girl." Devorah did, realizing she'd gone too far. "And you'd to well to watch your tongue, and see that your sister does as well." He lowered his voice. "Unless you'd like the King to learn of your history."

This time when he walked away, she let him.

Would you be the one to tell him? she wanted to ask. But what did it matter? This was the way of things for the thirteenth tribe; unless she was willing to risk Leorah's life as well as her own, she had no choice but to accept it.

Ahead, the tribes were beginning to gather. A bell was rung, and Devorah, thinking surely Leorah would come for the start of the traverse, went along with nearly every man, woman, and child in the camp. Even the crew of Sukru's galleon were at hand, watching as several dozen riders galloped across the sand, loosening the limbs of their grand akhalas. Each tribe had ten or twelve riders entering the race. The crimson manes of Tribe Narazid were the easiest to spot as they sprinted over the dunes. The riders of Tribe Rafik rode their akhalas hard, most standing in their saddles with their shamshirs raised high, as if they rode for war. The riders of Tribe Okan, however, were putting on a show. Their riders worked in unison as they galloped over the sand. Like a weave of threads, they traded positions, showing mastery of their horses, and their horses' mastery of teamwork. Annam's Traverse had only one winner, but Tribe Okan, working in concert, often filled the most positions in the race's second contest, improving their chances of securing one or even both positions in the race's third and final contest.

And then there was Kirhan. Now that she could see his akhala properly, it was much more impressive. It looked to be a full hand taller than any of the other horses preparing to take the traverse. It was well muscled. Its silver coat gleamed in the morning sun. One might wonder if it could withstand the harshness of the desert race, but it galloped with an eagerness, as if it had long been waiting to test its mettle against the mounts of the Great Shangazi.

After a time, Şelal mounted her own horse. The other shaikhs did the same. As was custom, they would ride with the champions for a time, and then let the race continue. Dozens of others from all tribes would follow a respectful distance behind them, a grand opening to the legendary race.

Pulling a whip from her saddle, Şelal cracked it over her head several times. "Riders!" she called. "To me!"

Devorah still saw no sign of Leorah. It worried her greatly. Leorah loved horses. Loved riding them. She'd want to see this. But in all likelihood she couldn't bear to see the start of a race that would give up their ring, one of the handful of things their mother had left them. And then another, all too real possibility occurred to her, a thing she dearly hoped she was wrong about.

Please, Leorah. Please don't be so foolish as that.

The riders gathered. Each was announced by Şelal. Their respective tribes whooped and shouted as the riders lined up along the top of a dune, some to Şelal's right, others to her left. The reception for some was naturally louder than others. Past champions, young hopefuls who'd proven themselves in their own tribe but not in the traverse, received tumultuous roars, prayers for the gods to rain favor down upon them.

There was Alize, a short, fierce woman of Okan who wore a patch over her left eye. Urdman, a rangy Narazid who'd won two traverses in the past, and Ornük, his son, whose introduction was nearly as loud as his father's had been. Rafik's most skilled riders were Şelal and Armesh's son, Benan, and a woman named Derya who was thrice Devorah's age but also thrice the rider.

Kirhan came last. Polite applause spread over the gathered crowd, there and gone in little time. The crew of Sukru's ship did no more than smile, and Sukru himself watched with bored impatience, as if the outcome was never in doubt and he was ready to take his winnings and set sail for Sharakhai.

The mood of the crowd was eager as Kirhan moved into line with the rest. They were ready to burst into a combined shout of approval, encouragement, celebration and joy. But then there came from behind the crowd a *hiyaah!* followed by the plodding sound of galloping hooves. Devorah knew before she came into view who it was; she hadn't even needed the rider's shout to know it was Leorah.

She rode a copper akhala, with a spear held high above her head. She rode crouched in the saddle with perfect form, just as their father had taught them. Devorah tried in vain to intercept her. Leorah saw and easily guided the horse wide while skirting the massive gathering. She rode out onto open sand, then guided her horse onto the path where the riders of the traverse would soon spill forth. With a grunt and a blurring sling of her right arm, she lofted the spear toward the distant line—the ancient desert symbol for a challenge, be it single combat or tribes going to war with one another.

The spear plunged deep into the sand. Leorah rode until she was just short of it, then reined her horse to a stop and called with a voice brimming with pride, "I would ride as well, Şelal Ymine'ala al Rafik! I would compete for the winnings on offer!"

Şelal urged her horse into a walk, leaving the long line of riders behind. Devorah could not see her well, but she looked incensed, her face red with anger. "You think *you* can compete in the traverse?"

"I do."

"You've not been given leave."

"I am my own woman." Leorah's horse was eager. It stamped its hooves on the sand as it turned. Leorah reined it over to face Şelal once more. "The traverse is open to all, is it not? Ehmel was to compete before he broke his leg on the journey here. Let me take his place."

There was a stirring in the gathering behind Şelal. Leorah's request was not unreasonable. The race was open to all. But the other tribes didn't know Şelal like Devorah did. They hadn't seen her darker side.

"What you say is true," Şelal said loudly, "but all those gathered here sit atop their own steeds. What I see before me"—she flung a dramatic wave toward Leorah, as if she were arguing before a tribunal—"is a woman who *stole* a horse to ride in this race."

Leorah rode back and forth, her face stern, committed. "This is a horse of Tribe Rafik, and *I* am of Tribe Rafik! *I* am a Biting Shield. Might I not ride one of the tribe's horses to lift our honor higher?"

Sand and stone, Leorah was *daring* Şelal to reveal her true heritage. Şelal might be angry enough to do it, but if she did, *she* would be implicated as well. The days of the Kings' actively hunting those of the thirteenth tribe might be past, but they'd hardly stand by and allow one to pass beneath their noses, nor would they allow a shaikh to knowingly harbor them.

"That is a horse of Tribe Rafik, it is true, but alas, dear Leorah, it has not been prepared for the traverse. You know by now the horses are selected weeks ahead of time. That they are trained daily, just as the riders are, for the rigors of this race. I will not jeopardize a single akhala because you, on a whim, have judged yourself worthy to ride beside the champions of the west."

Back and forth Leorah rode, suddenly unsure of herself. She might have called for Ehmel's horse, but it had turned up lame in the same accident that had seen Ehmel's leg broken. "Tribe Rafik!" she called loudly. "Some of your horses have been conditioned. Will none of you lend me your steed to run this race?" Leorah knew the answer as well as Devorah did. The tribe had accepted her at Şelal's request, but they all knew Leorah was not one of them. None would answer her call. Yet Leorah rode on, refusing to give in. She plucked the spear from where it lay in the sand. "None of you?"

As she galloped across the dune, she raised the spear high. Her bearing was proud, and all the more desperate for it—it was as sad a display as Devorah had ever seen.

Şelal looked on with satisfaction. Sukru watched with a hunger, as if he wished this all to end in bloodshed.

But then a voice rang out, "She may ride one of mine."

Voices filled the warming desert air with a low murmur. All eyes turned to the end of the line of horses, where Kirhan stood tall in his saddle.

"I've two more that were trained," he called out, loud and clear. "She may ride the one of her choice."

Everyone turned to Şelal, who stared at Kirhan with a stony expression. Her eyes, however, were ablaze. "She is of *my* tribe."

"And she wishes to ride," Kirhan said flatly. "So let her."

Şelal looked to Sukru, who had been watching this unexpected development with a look as sour as Malasani limes. His only response was to flick one hand toward Kirhan in assent. There was nothing for Şelal to do, not without looking the fool.

"How very gracious," she said to Kirhan in a dead tone. "Quickly then. We've a race to run."

As Kirhan waved to the Sharakhani gathering, two horses were led forward. Devorah ran over the sand to her sister, who was just then dismounting. "What have you *done*?" Devorah rasped.

"I'm sorry, Devorah. I cannot let it pass." She strode purposefully toward where Kirhan was now dropping to the sand and accepting the reins of his two spare horses.

"Don't let her do this," Devorah said to him quietly as the three of them met.

Kirhan looked at her, then Leorah. "She is a woman grown. She can do as she wishes." He turned his gaze purposefully on the two horses. "You can take one as well, should you wish."

"You're smitten," Devorah replied. "I can see it in you. But I tell you now, what you do places my sister in grave danger."

"Oh?" He held the reins, one in each hand, toward Leorah. "And why would that be? Is your sister like to die in the desert?"

"It's not to do with her *riding*."

"Well, I'd judge you have about as much time as it takes tea to steep to tell me what it *is* to do with."

Leorah, her face grim, had been inspecting both horses—one a bay stallion with a coat so rich it shone like molten iron against the brightness of the sun, the other a mare with a speckled coat that looked like pearls spilled over a pile of powdered kohl. Both were already saddled and provisioned with food and water for the trek ahead.

Devorah fumed, but what was there to say? She could hardly reveal their secrets to the King's man, and Leorah knew it. She had the upper hand, and was using it to leave the camp with a chance at winning back the prize their mother had left to them.

Devorah could think of only one thing that might change Leorah's mind. She nearly confessed it, the secret that had been burning inside her since they'd fled here to Tribe Rafik. But how could she? She couldn't, not in front of Kirhan. So she held her tongue and watched as Leorah accepted the reins of the stallion.

Leorah hugged Devorah close. "Forgive me," she said, then began leading the horse away.

Devorah had never felt so helpless, not even when her parents and brother had been murdered. She said to Leorah's back, "You're a selfish little girl, sister."

Leorah answered without turning. "Selfish, perhaps, but selfish for the both of us."

Moments later she and Kirhan were mounted and lined up with the rest of riders. Şelal cracked her whip three times, and then they were off, the champions and those who would accompany them, leaving Devorah to watch their forms dwindle into the distance.

On the fourth day of the traverse, as true night fell across the desert, Leorah rode Kirhan's stallion toward a large oasis. She'd left in such a rush she hadn't even learned the horse's name, but she'd taken to calling him Wadi for the way he liked to ride in the troughs between the dunes. Now that they were close, she kicked Wadi into a trot. He tugged at the reins once or twice but complied, perhaps as eager to reach the oasis as she was.

Tulathan was high in the sky, a beaten silver coin against a bed of broken diamonds. The oasis was a welcome sight, but Tulathan's light made it look lonely and forgotten, a scene from the children's tales where wights hid just out of sight, ready to prey on the living who arrived to partake of the cool water. The thought sent chills down her spine. A moment later, however, a warm feeling drove away the fear, for it also reminded her of the times her father had taken her and Devorah to swim. The desert's bright sun, how she missed them. Holding baba's bearlike hand. Making rosemary flat-bread with memma. Chasing her brother between the dunes. She was so exhausted from the days of riding that a small part of her hoped they'd step out from behind one of the trees.

A moment later, she nearly shivered out of her skin as a viper skittered out from under a desert fern. She held the reins tight as Wadi's head jerked back and his tail flicked. He danced from the snake's path as it twisted with surprising speed into the sand. Guiding

Wadi around the edge of the oasis, she finally spied three forms huddling close around a fire. Beyond the fire, horses were tied to a rope. A large tent stood, its flaps fluttering in the cool breeze. Many small tents were pitched in a row beyond it, waiting for riders to take their rest.

This was the first of the contest's two waypoints, a place where every rider's passage was recorded, thereby ensuring that all were following the prescribed path. The second waypoint was a standing stone so remote from reliable sources of water that those who didn't carefully plan their food, water, path, and pace back to camp risked not only their standing in the traverse but their own lives and the lives of their horses.

As far as Leorah knew, she was the first to arrive. She'd forgone any delays by skipping the smaller oases on the way, choosing instead to push and reach this oasis early, rest for as long as she could and, if her luck held, move on before anyone saw her.

Old Khyrn was the judge from Tribe Rafik. Noticing Leorah's arrival, he stood and limped his way toward her. "Well met, friend. Come. Sit by the fire awhile. Take a sip of araq if you like." The words were cordial, meant for any rider who might have come, but when Leorah slid down from Wadi's saddle and approached, Khyrn's eyes went wide, then thinned. "Why are *you* here?"

Leorah allowed her annoyance to add bite to her words. "I was out for a bit of a ride when I saw the oasis. Thought I'd harvest some dates before moving on."

Annoyance mixed with the distrust in Khyrn's eyes. "Don't sass."

"Then don't ask fool questions!"

"You weren't on the list of champions the day I left!"

"What matter is that? Şelal allowed me to race. So I am."

The others by the fire, a woman from Tribe Okan and a man from Narazid—each only a handful of years older than Leorah—watched the exchange with amusement. Cheeks rosy, smiles easy, they looked as though they'd had more than their fair share of araq already.

"It's only strange is all," Khyrn went on.

"Are all not welcome in the race?"

"Now, see, welcome's a funny word," Khyrn replied. "There are times when we welcome friends. And times when we welcome our enemies as well." He glanced back at the other two. "Is it not so?"

Before either could respond, Leorah—still working out the leagues of riding from her bones—limped straight up to Khyrn and poked him hard in the chest. "Are you calling me your *enemy*, Khyrn Rellana'ala?"

Khyrn's eyes went wide, as if he had no idea why she was acting in such a way. "No!" He turned awkwardly and motioned to the fire, a bumbling attempt at welcoming her to share in its warmth. "It's true, though, isn't it?" He nearly tripped over a rock as Leorah led Wadi past him.

Leorah tied Wadi to the long rope running between two palms, leaving more than enough slack so he could drink from the nearby water. Then she unsaddled him and returned to the fire and settled herself down, exhausted. The aches and pains from days of riding returned with a fury, but the fire felt good. So good that, though she was amongst strangers, she unwound her turban and let her long hair fall down around her shoulders. Khyrn tried to make chit-chat. He asked about the start of the traverse, how it was Leorah had come to join it. He was friendly enough after his strange greeting, but Leorah still harbored the feeling that she'd always be an outsider to Tribe Rafik, and answered only in clipped responses.

The two lovebirds sat whispering, leaning into one another, knees touching. Leorah was curious about them, curious for news from the other tribes as well, but they were well and truly smitten. Their words were whispers. Their eyes were only for one another. Soon they were standing, bowing a pleasant night, and heading for the water, hand in hand. As they neared the water's edge, they quickened their pace and splashed into the pool, giddy as children.

"Well," Khyrn said a short while later. "I'm off for a bit of sleep. Wake me if more come, won't you?"

Leorah nodded, and Khyrn toddled away in that strange gait of his, leaving her alone. For a time she merely breathed the night air and listened to the riot of insects chittering and buzzing around her. She might have heard a giggle coming from the water. A pleasant silence followed, but it was broken by the distant sound of grunting, then muffled cries of passion, and finally by the woman crying, "Lai, lai, lai!" as if she were going to war.

The two of them laughed immediately after, and Leorah chuckled to herself. *War of another sort...*

The sort the desert *should* foster instead of constantly feeding the sands of the Great Mother with battle and blood.

As the sounds of lovemaking faded, a great lethargy overcame her. *I should be sleeping already.* She knew there was little time to spare. She needed to be ready to leave before sunrise. "But I would drink of the night," she said to the darkling sky. "Can you see it as well, baba?" She hoped her father, who'd given her and Devorah their love of the night, might be standing on the farther shores, watching a sky not so different from this one.

I should be sleeping.

But the peace of the expansive sky over an oasis after four days of hard riding felt not merely welcome, but necessary. She ached all over. Her crotch felt like a mule had kicked it. She had blisters along her thighs and rump, though she'd done her best to tend to them on the few short breaks she'd allowed herself. Now it was all catching up to her.

As if her fears had been given life by the desert gods, there came the sound of plodding hooves. Slowly, it emerged from the darkness: a tall beast with a coat of molten silver, fetlocks of wrought iron and a mane to match. The horse's large, round eyes glittered in the firelight. Beside the akhala was Kirhan, who matched the majesty of the beast in every way.

Bloody gods, he doesn't look the least bit tired. How can that be?

He continued past the fire to tie up his horse to the same rope where Wadi and the judges' horses were resting. He unsaddled him, ran his hands along his neck, whispered to him awhile. He even pulled out a small, dried apple and fed it to the tall beast. He had another for Wadi. Both horses nickered, tossing their heads back, then huffed, the two of them nuzzling one another.

As they did, Kirhan wet a towel and began to wipe away the dried froth that had built up along his horse's neck and chest during the day. Leorah should have done the same, and now she felt thoughtless for how she'd treated Wadi. She levered herself back to her feet and wet a towel of her own. Kirhan didn't overtly watch her, but she could feel his attention on her as she rubbed the dried sweat from his coat.

When she was done, she scratched behind Wadi's ears. "I'm sorry," she whispered. Wadi didn't seem impressed. Still, she rubbed his coat awhile longer, and he didn't object.

"My thanks," Kirhan said as they sat by the fire.

"It wasn't for you." She held out the nearly full bottle of araq Khyrn had left.

"Even so." He took a short swallow, though it seemed more out of custom than any desire to partake in it. After stoppering the bottle, he held it out for Leorah. When she declined he set it carefully beside him on the sand. "He doesn't really need it." He glanced over at the horses. "I've been training them for races like this since they were born."

"*You* trained them?"

For the first time, a smile cracked Kirhan's weary features. "You're surprised?"

"It's only… I thought you merely rode them."

His muscular shoulders lifted in an exaggerated shrug, as if he were so physically inclined, so accustomed to economy of movement, that he was combining his reply with an attempt at working out the kinks from the journey without even realizing it. "My father was a horse trainer. I took to it early."

"How many do you train?"

"Only the three."

"No more?"

"I would like to one day. I've had offers from several lords and ladies in Sharakhai. But my duties for my Lord King led me elsewhere."

"Duties… Some would call it stealing glory from the tribes."

Kirhan drew one arm across his chest and hugged it close with the opposite. "Some would say the desert tribes have glory to spare."

"Some in Sharakhai, you mean."

He switched arms, wincing as he drew the other close. "Where else?"

Leorah snorted. "Well, some say the Kings should leave well enough alone. You have your *own* customs. Leave us to ours."

"It may surprise you to learn, Leorah of Tribe Rafik, that it wasn't my Lord King's idea to come here to *steal your glory*."

At this, Leorah laughed. "Come now... You seem a wise enough man. You can't possibly believe such a story."

"It's no story. Your shaikh, Şelal, sent a messenger months ago, offering the amethyst ring to him."

Leorah's words died on her lips. "She *offered* it?"

"Just so. Your messenger said that, having learned of his desire for baubles that might possess some magic, Şelal had a prize that would likely interest him greatly."

"So, just like that"—she snapped her fingers over her head—"she offered him the jewel?"

"No. Not *just like that*. There was the traverse to consider."

"That makes no sense. Why would she force Sukru to race for it?"

"How would *I* know? I'm just a man who trains horses." He got to his feet, somewhat less gracefully than when he'd sat down. "One final thing. Your horse, Alir, was trained for this, as I said, but you cannot maintain the pace you set on the way here. I would feel poorly if you died of thirst, but I would never forgive you if you killed Alir over a simple refusal to grant him rest. Watch for the signs."

Wadi *had* been showing signs of exhaustion. She'd noticed them near dusk and still she'd pushed. In that moment, she realized something that shamed her to such a degree that she could no longer hold Kirhan's gaze. As her eyes drifted to the fire, the realization hit her full force; she'd been treating Wadi as if he were the King's property and nothing more, as if he were *expendable*, because what did it matter if a King lost some small portion of his vast wealth? Wadi hadn't deserved that.

"Did you hear me?" Kirhan asked, his face angry.

"Yes," she replied, "I know the signs."

"Name them."

She ticked them off on her fingers. "Sides heaving. Flared nostrils. Head down more often than not. Sweating. Frothing along the neck, belly, chest and flank. And if it gets bad, cotton mouth, lack of sweat, a loss of desire to drink or eat. They can wander, dizzily. Or they might lay down and refuse to get up."

He looked surprised, as though he'd been expecting a different response. "Yes. Many horses will slow or refuse to go on when they're exhausted, but know that I've trained Alir to push if need be. He still fights at the reins, though. He's done so with you?"

She nodded, embarrassed to admit it.

He nodded back, then ambled toward the distant row of tents, those meant for the riders. "Keep him safe," he said, and ducked inside the nearest.

Before going to her own tent, Leorah walked along the edge of the nearby pool and dug up several sweet desert yams she'd noted on the ride in. She washed them and then fed them to Wadi, one by one. She sang a song and brushed his shoulders as he ate. "Don't worry," she said when he'd finished. "I'll keep you safe."

Wadi snorted and clawed one hoof against the sandy earth. After one last pat, she went to her own tent and slept.

When Leorah woke the next morning, Kirhan was already gone. Several other riders had come in while she slept. She moved quietly, so as not to rouse them. After refilling the three water skins each rider was allowed, then urging Wadi to drink his fill one last time—an offer he refused—she was off.

As the oasis dwindled behind her, she leaned forward and rubbed Wadi's neck. "Alir is a stupid name. While *I* ride you, your name will be Wadi. What say you? Do you like it?" Wadi made no sort of reply, but for her that was as good as assent. She patted his shoulder. "That's a good boy."

She followed the hoof prints Kirhan's silver akhala had left, but as she continued, the trail faded, which meant he'd set a hard pace toward the second waypoint—harder than *she* was setting, in any case. She didn't care. The day was already miserably hot, and Wadi was listless. She wanted to give him a chance to recover. And besides, they had time to spare; she only needed to be in the first ten in order to reach the second contest.

Before high sun, another rider, the tough-as-leather Derya of Tribe Rafik, rode past her. Only a few hours after that, as Leorah was staking a sun shade into the sand so she and Wadi could rest during the day's hottest hours, the tower of a man they called Urdman, and his son, Ornük, came riding past.

"Share my shade?" Leorah asked.

"We have our own," Urdman replied, and they

pitched theirs a quarter league ahead, as if they needed the comfort of moving beyond her before they would stop and give themselves respite from the heat.

"Stubborn," Leorah said to their wavering image. "We don't need them anyway, do we, Wadi?"

He thumped one hoof against the sand.

Wadi's spiritless pace continued throughout the following days. He wasn't the same horse he'd been on the ride to the oasis. His belly began to rumble every so often, at times sounding like stones were tumbling inside him. She worried she'd done something terrible, something he wouldn't recover from.

"Please don't die on me, boy. I've only just met you."

The akhala were efficient beasts, prized across the whole of the desert. They could go several weeks without proper food. A bit of ironweed or a nibble on firebrush was enough to sustain them, as long as they started with a good bit of fat, which they collected around their chest and shoulders and rump. As for water, as long as you didn't force them into a gallop too often, they could go for many days with very little. Even so, Leorah went out of her way to steer their path toward patches of bushes so Wadi could graze.

One day while doing so, she saw two more riders

trot past in the distance. She reached the second waypoint near sunset on her sixth day out from the oasis. After checking in with the observers, she immediately pushed on. The sense of urgency was returning now that the end of the race was nearing. But Wadi's listlessness continued. As did the angry sounds in his belly.

Three more riders, their horses all displaying the bright red manes of Tribe Narazid, passed her the following day. A fourth rider, Alize from Tribe Okan, followed hours later. She guided her copper akhala close, and stared at both Wadi and Leorah. She looked grim with the patch covering her left eye, but Leorah realized shortly after she'd misjudged the woman. It was only concern for a fellow rider.

"Is your horse ill?" Alize asked when she came near.

"A bit," Leorah admitted, patting Wadi's neck. "He only needs rest, I think."

"Do you wish to ride with me?" she asked, motioning to her own saddle.

Accepting the offer would mean giving up on the traverse, and Leorah wasn't ready to do that just yet. "My heart sings at your generosity, but no."

It wasn't so simple as merely continuing the race, however. In eleventh place, she was currently out of the running, and in the distance behind her, she saw the wavering forms of several more riders.

She jogged by Wadi's side that whole day, sipping sparingly on her water, and giving a healthy portion to Wadi though he likely didn't need it so soon after the oasis. The pace she set for herself was grueling, but being riderless seemed to help Wadi's disposition. As the sun was lowering in the west, however, he simply stopped. He would go no further despite her tugging at his reins. Two more riders rode past without a word as she stood before Wadi, running her hands slowly along his muzzle. Wadi eyed the other horses. He shook his mane and nickered, perhaps ashamed that by delaying, they were effectively giving up the race.

"It's not your fault," Leorah said. "It's mine. The gods are punishing me for my arrogance."

Was it the grasses she'd fed him before the oasis? Or the yams? Or perhaps Wadi had picked up a case of threadworm at the oasis. The worms usually only infected foals, but adults were occasionally stricken as well.

She wondered why the gods wished to prevent her from winning back her mother's ring. Did the ring mean something to them? Or were they merely protecting the interests of King Sukru, a man they'd already bestowed many blessings upon? Or perhaps it was as simple as scripture. *Thou shalt not covet the material over the spiritual.* Isn't that what the Al'ambra said?

"We'll get you back to Kirhan, yes?" She stroked Wadi's neck. "He'll know what to do."

Exactly when she'd fallen asleep, she couldn't recall, but in the morning, she was awoken by Wadi's pained whinnying. He was walking in a circle, but his pace was strange and uneven. His eyes were rolling back in their sockets and he was tossing his head up and down. He looked possessed, his tack jingling, the reins slapping against his shoulders.

She'd already removed his saddle, but now she took off his bridle as well. She prayed another rider would come. She'd been foolish to deny Alize. She'd gladly take up the offer now. But no one came, and she started to wonder if she'd gone off course the prior evening.

Wadi started to buck and kick.

"I'm so sorry, boy!" She tried to approach, to console him, but each time she tried Wadi skittered away. "I don't know what to do!"

Then Wadi went still. He began to make soil, and she realized she'd seen him do so only once since leaving the oasis. It kept coming in large, wet clumps, thumping against the sand. He pissed while doing so. On and on it went. Breath of the desert, she'd never seen so much come out of a horse at once. Wadi stepped forward, shivered as if he were plagued by stinging flies, then passed even more.

When he was done, he plodded forward and stood still as a statue. His breath was coming in great huffs. Leorah walked toward him slowly, arms spread wide, worried she might scare him. But Wadi didn't shy away. He leaned into her touch. And then of a sudden he reared onto his back hooves. He dropped and galloped forward, then reared and charged again, neighing this time.

He circled her once, twice, throwing his head back, as if he had no idea what to do with this fount of energy. He came near her, nudging her with his shoulder.

"You want water?" She offered some to him from a treated leather bag meant for the purpose. He lapped some of it up, but then threw his head back and skipped away. He circled her again, then used his muzzle to push his reins along the sand.

Leorah laughed. "You want to race?"

Wadi stood proud, waiting.

"Very well," she said, and saddled him with a wary sort of hope, the sort you don't look square in the eye lest you scare it off.

Then they were riding. Wadi was tentative at first.

Several times, he passed a large amount of gas. Each time Leorah wondered if what she was doing was wise. But then the discomfort seemed to vanish, and Wadi was running with a power she hadn't seen since the first days of the traverse.

No, she realized. *It's well more than those early days.*

Wadi was like an unbroken colt, powering over the sand as if eager to reassert his dominance over the Great Mother. Ahead, flitting in and out of view as the heat wavered, were three riders. Wadi closed the distance over several hours of steadfast cantering. When they came near, he leaned into a full gallop. They tried to keep pace, but Wadi would not be denied. He pushed past them as if they were standing still.

Leorah laughed. She unwound her turban and stood in the saddle and waved it over her head. In those moments, she *was* those rolling dunes. She was a powerful horse, a limitless sky, and joy unfiltered. Even so, she knew her ability to reach the second contest was in jeopardy. She recognized none of the riders from the days since the oasis, which meant she still had ground to make up. How much, she wasn't sure, but she knew the end of the race was near.

The mountains lay ahead, an ochre smear along the horizon. All riders would be pushing hard. Likely

Kirhan and the other leaders had already crossed the finish line near camp, securing their place in the second contest. She decided to rest only a short while that night. But she'd hardly fallen asleep when she heard riders trotting over the sand. She got up and walked Wadi, refusing to push him too hard, refusing as well to risk injury by riding during the moonless hours of the night.

At the first sign of light, she returned to the saddle. Black mountains now loomed.

"Let's run, shall we?" she said to Wadi. "Let's run like the autumn wind!"

Wadi huffed. He shook his mane. Then they were riding hard over the soft sand. Ahead, she saw a cluster of riders. She was slowly catching up to them, but she could also see a great ring of ships and the camp that lay between them. The finish was only the turn of a clock away.

Wadi seemed to realize it too. He struck a pace none of the other horses in the traverse—including, she was certain, Kirhan's silver gelding—could match.

She caught up to the rearmost rider, slid past him as the sound of the crowd ahead rose above the pounding of hooves. Of the ten yellow pennants that would have been hung to indicate how many places were available for the traverse's second contest, only three remained. They hung from a wooden post that had been staked into the sand. As a horse galloped past, its rider, Alize, raised her arms triumphantly, and another pennant was taken down.

Gods, only two remain, and there are six riders still ahead!

Leorah was crouched in her stirrups, holding the reins in both hands, her body moving in perfect sync with Wadi's flow. She let Wadi choose his own path through the strange dunes. Most riders rode up and down, straight toward the finish, but Wadi flew along the troughs. It took them a bit wide, but the even ground allowed him a greater pace.

They passed two more riders, while in the distance, another Bloody Mane was crossing the finish line, leaving only one yellow pennant to swing from the post.

Three riders were still ahead of Leorah. Wadi galloped on, an undeniable force. She passed one rider. The next tried to steer into Wadi's path to slow him down, but Wadi cut to the opposite side in a perfect display of instincts and training and raw, unbridled power.

Past the rider they swept, and drove up the final slope.

Leorah's heart fell when she saw how much distance she still needed to close on the last rider. She was sure she'd lost, but then realized how badly the rider's horse was flagging. He'd pushed too hard, too soon, and now his horse couldn't keep the pace.

On Wadi went, hurtling toward the finish.

Moments before crossing, they burst ahead of the final rider. The crowd roared. Horns sounded and drums played. And the final pennant was taken down.

Later that day, with the revels of the first contest in full swing, Devorah strode toward King Sukru's camp, which was arrayed behind his galleon. The central pavilion and the surrounding tents were situated in such a way that the ship's bulk shielded them from the view of the three gathered camps, as if Sukru couldn't bear to look upon the sullied masses of the desert tribes.

Leorah would be incensed. No doubt she still would be when the revels were over. Devorah *ought* to be incensed, but each step she took toward the pavilion only gnawed at the hollow feeling inside her. It felt as if the pavilion's entrance were a great, slavering maw, and here she was, trudging toward it like the dolorous amberlark from the children's tales, the one that had been tricked into stepping into the hyena's mouth.

The hyena had laughed with its brothers after. *And such a pretty meal it was.*

Two Blade Maidens stood at attention at the pavilion's entrance. They wore black battle dresses and turbans and ebon blades at their sides. The veils of their turbans concealed their faces, their emotions. Such was the dispassion in their kohl-rimmed eyes, however, that Devorah suspected they'd give nothing away even if their veils had been hanging loose.

She came to a stop before them, waiting awkwardly. When neither gave greeting, she said, "I was summoned by King Sukru."

The leftmost Maiden sketched a mocking bow. "Well, why didn't you say so, *Biting Shield?*"

Devorah wasn't sure how to respond. Staring at Devorah, she laughed derisively, flicked her hand toward the entrance, then pretended Devorah didn't exist.

Squeezing past them, Devorah stepped inside the pavilion to find a half-dozen braziers burning brightly, lighting the underside of the roof's fine canvas like the center of a pearl must look from within.

A handful of servants moved about. One was using

mortar and pestle with a galloping rhythm to grind kahve beans. Another was making elaborate, golden drinks made of araq, spices, and finely chopped dragonfruit. King Sukru's vizira, a comely woman with a broad, knowing smile, was bowed low near the King himself, who sat on a mound of pillows on the far side of a low table. When the vizira noticed Devorah, she stood and tipped her head pleasantly. The servants, all young men who looked eerily similar to the vizira—her sons?—did as well.

"Please," the vizira said, motioning to the pillows opposite Sukru.

The hollow feeling in Devorah's chest deepened as she complied. She wanted to leave. She wanted to run away with Leorah, find a new place in the desert to hide. But what could she do? "A thousand gratitudes for inviting me to dine, my Lord King."

Sukru flicked one hand, much as the Blade Maiden had done a only a moment ago. "Even the Kings of Sharakhai must eat. Is it not so?"

"Of course, my Lord King."

"You like mint-and-lemon lamb?"

The air was thick with the scent of it. Normally, Devorah's mouth would be watering, but there in the pavilion, sitting as she was before the Reaping King, her mouth was dry as desert sage. She replied with as much enthusiasm as she could muster. "I do, Excellence. Very much so."

Sukru seemed to sneer while weighing those words, but then he looked up to his vizira and nodded. The woman made a circling motion with one finger. Immediately, and with accustomed ease, the servants worked in flawless concert to deliver several small courses. They ate of savory crackers with caramelized onions and fresh, herbed cheese whose aftertaste delivered a pleasant tang that was strangely similar to the horse milk cheese Tribe Rafik often made. They had greens with wine-laced sausage, pomegranate seeds that burst with flavor, and a carrot-and-sweet-turnip dressing that, despite Devorah's nervousness, made her mouth water with every bite. The promised lamb came next, savory meat that melted off the bone and whose juices mixed with the fluffy, perfectly cooked rice.

Devorah had never eaten a better meal, yet she enjoyed none of it. She was constantly looking to Sukru, wondering when he'd get to his purpose in summoning her here.

To finish, they had freshly brewed kahve and rosemary-cream biscuits that were so delicate they felt impossible here in the harshness of the desert.

"You like it?" Sukru asked.

"Of course, my Lord King."

Sukru gave her a knowing nod. "You wouldn't know it from the way you keep glaring at me. I'm not preparing to chop your head off, girl."

In truth, she hadn't been thinking that, but she certainly was now. *Such a pretty meal it was…* "Of course not, Excellence."

Sukru stared more intently, perhaps waiting for her attitude to change, but how could it? This was all so strange. She felt as if she'd been caught in slipsand, and that every moment that passed was pulling her deeper and deeper. Soon enough she'd be lost to the world, and no one would be the wiser.

While Leorah—the gods damn her—is off dancing with handsome Kirhan.

Finally, Sukru had had enough. He huffed a breath and waved everyone out. They left in a rush, closing the front and rear tent flaps behind them, leaving Sukru and Devorah alone in the pavilion. From the table he picked up a blue bottle that had yet to be touched. Into fresh glasses he poured two healthy servings of araq. He took his up and sipped, waving for Devorah to do the same.

Devorah complied, if only to humor him, but by

the gods who breathe, the araq tasted like sunshine. There were notes of pear and persimmon and peach, with undercurrents of distant campfires, veiled beyond the dunes. It did much to lift Devorah's spirits.

"I thought you might like it," Sukru said, sipping his own drink with relish. "It's from the northeast, the land of the Standing Stones. Years ago I might have scoffed at the notion, but they've managed to fold in several Mirean ingredients to good effect."

"They have," Devorah echoed. "It's better than any araq I've ever had. Any *drink* I've ever had."

"I'm not surprised," he said. "A single bottle costs as much as an akhala." He finished his drink and poured himself another before speaking again. "The other day, when the prizes of Annam's Traverse were announced, your sister had what is known in Sharakhai as *widow's shock*."

Devorah wasn't quite sure she understood all the implications of the idiom, but the heart of it was plain enough. Leorah had not handled the situation with aplomb. "She was only surprised, my Lord King. I hope you'll forgive her."

"Mmm." He swished a mouthful of araq around both cheeks, then swallowed. "And you? Were *you* surprised?"

"Yes, I was."

"Why?"

"Because that ring belonged to my mother." There was no sense denying it. He would surely have heard the tale by now.

"And what happened to her, your mother?"

"She died in a sandstorm along with my father, uncle, and two cousins." A necessary lie, one she, Leorah, Armesh, and Şelal had all agreed to when they'd been allowed into Tribe Rafik.

"A pity," Sukru replied. "And the gemstone…" He said the words casually, though for a man like Sukru, who always seemed like a jackal working up the courage to attack, it seemed immediately threatening. "The amethyst your sister now competes for. How was it that it came into Şelal's possession if, as you say, your mother was lost in a sandstorm?"

"She rarely wore it. It was kept in a box, which was where it remained until we finally accepted that none of them would return."

"A pity," he said again, though this time the words were worse than lifeless. They were practically *amused*. "She wore it seldom, you said, but I wonder, did she ever tell you of its properties?"

Devorah shook her head, hoping that in her silence,

the King might tell her more. “Properties, Excellence?”

“Have you worn it yourself?”

“Sometimes, as a child.”

“And what did you feel at those times?”

She shrugged, suddenly more curious than fearful. “I felt proud, like a queen of the desert. Leorah and I used to play—”

Sukru waved her words away like a bothersome cloud of flies. “What did you feel *inside*?”

“Forgive me, my King, I’m not sure—”

“The tribes trade for information, do they not?” The King’s eyes had grown sharp, revealing some small amount of the anger that seemed to be bubbling up inside him. “While we drink, let us do so.”

Coming from a King, and she but a woman from a distant desert tribe, the words were indistinguishable from an edict. “Of course,” she replied. “What I have is yours.”

“You know the story of how Yerinde swept Tulathan from the heavens?”

“All know that story, my Lord King.”

“Yes, but what is rarely spoken of is the manner in which she was taken.”

“She was ensorcelled,” Devorah said.

“True enough, but how? When Iri left our world

for the farther fields, he bequeathed to Yerinde, his favorite among the younger gods, a gem. An amethyst of astounding size and clarity. Some called it the Sunset Stone. Others the Flame of Iri. Yerinde used it to trap Tulathan, her soul caught within its facets. Thereafter, Yerinde returned to her tower in the mountains and secreted the gem away, hoping to woo the silver goddess over time, to make Tulathan love her as *she* loved Tulathan. For many long years, they spoke at sunset and sunrise—such was the power inherent in the stone—but always Tulathan resisted Yerinde's advances.

"Meanwhile, Tulathan's sister, Rhia, grew despondent. She searched the desert wide for her twin, to no avail. Then one day, many years later, the fates rewarded her persistence. Goezhen, who'd learned of Yerinde's whereabouts, had whispered it not to his fellow gods, but to his children, the ehrekh, crafted from his own blood, his own hatred of man. Through them, Rhia learned that it was Yerinde who'd taken Tulathan away.

"Enraged, she went to Yerinde's tower and struck the goddess down. She shattered the amethyst, freeing her sister in the process. The stone was broken into four pieces. They became known as Iri's Four Sacred Stones. Some called them the Tears of Tulathan. One was taken by Tulathan herself, to remind her of her own imprisonment. A second was destroyed by Thaash centuries later. One is believed stolen and taken away from the desert a thousand years ago. That leaves the fourth, of which there has been no word for centuries." Sukru paused, staring intently at Devorah.

He was implying, of course, that her mother's amethyst was one of the four, a Sacred Stone of Iri.

"It cannot be," she said.

"Why can it not?"

"It was my mother's. A simple piece of jewelry."

"No one can look upon that stone and call it simple."

"Still. She wore it as if it were nothing more than a fancy."

"And where did she get it?"

"From my grandmother, her mother."

"And she?"

"I was never told."

"Come now. Surely your mother told you something of its nature."

"No," Devorah said, "she never did. Surely it cannot be the same stone!"

"When you wore it, did you feel a yearning of any sort, an emptiness while others were near?"

"I'm afraid I didn't, Your Grace."

To this point, Sukru had seemed eager, if piqued, at her inability to share more. Now, his expression darkened. *Such a pretty meal…* "Centuries ago it was considered not merely rude to withhold information once they'd entered a trade of knowledge, but unlawful. Men and women lost fingers for replying with less candor than their counterpart. Others, when it was important to the defense of Sharakhai, lost their heads."

"I wasn't aware we had entered into so formal a version of trading."

"Now you are."

Devorah knew what he wanted, but knew just as well she couldn't give it to him. Everything he'd said so far had been a revelation. It seemed impossible. How could such a stone have fallen into her mother's hands? She couldn't begin to guess, but she was well certain if she didn't tell Sukru *something*, there would be a price to pay.

She nearly confessed her secret, the one she hadn't even shared with Leorah yet. She only wanted to be free from this tent, free from Sukru. But instead, after thinking on it a moment, she took a different tack, a more dangerous one. "My mother told me nothing before her death. But I have worn the stone, as I've said, and I swear before the gods of the desert, I felt nothing at the time. I knew not what I held, however. If you know anything—anything at all—you could share it with me. Perhaps Şelal will allow me to wear it and I could tell you what I find."

Until now, everything about Sukru had spoken of his hunger for knowledge: the leer in his eyes, his insistent tone, the way his lips drew back to reveal his small, yellow teeth. A rage had been building in him, a thing he might unleash at any moment. At Devorah's suggestion, however, he seemed to shrink. His expression devolved into one of simple, childlike worry, of jealousy over secrets he clearly wanted to hoard as his own. He masked it a moment later, replacing it with an expression of simple neutrality, a sort of inoffensive airiness made all the more conspicuous for how desperate it made him seem to discover more about the amethyst. Were it anyone else sitting before her, she would have laughed.

Sukru sipped his araq, and the somewhat discourteous manner he'd displayed on her arrival returned. "There's no need," he replied with a wave of his hand. "You'll forgive, I trust, my curiosity getting the better of me." With his glass, the golden araq within it swirling, he motioned for Devorah to take up hers. "Please. To let any of this go unappreciated would be a high crime."

He became almost friendly over the next hour. Perhaps he realized he'd gone too far. Or perhaps he believed her story, that she knew nothing, and with that barrier removed found that he could talk to her as he would any other. Whatever the case, they spoke of Devorah's parents, sliding quickly to life in Sharakhai, the palaces, the cramped streets, the high walls. Devorah loved to sail, loved the feel of the wind as it filled a sandship's sails, loved the varied swaths of desert she'd visited in her young life, which had only fueled her fire to see more. It made his stories of Sharakhai feel like damnation, a sentence to life in an oubliette. The day she left the desert was the day she would die and fly to the farther fields.

After a veritable flock of bite-sized, thousand-layer sweets, the King said his farewells and Devorah was soon walking over the cooling sands toward the Rafik camp. She forced her pace to remain slow, calm, even after she'd moved beyond the galleon; there was no telling if one of the ship's crew or the Blade Maidens might see her. Once she'd moved beyond the first line of tents, however, she was running headlong along the unordered rows until she'd arrived at the tent she shared with Leorah.

Inside, she dropped to her knees before their wooden chest, the one where they kept their few valuables. She dumped them all out—handfuls of coins, bits of paper with poems written on them, small ivory statues—so that she could get to the bottom, which was false. Pulling back the wood, a compartment was revealed, and in it, a small silk pouch. She pulled the drawstrings to widen the mouth, then upended it.

What fell from within was a golden ring with an amethyst set in it. It was the same size as the one they'd given to Şelal, and nearly identical save for the crack that could barely be seen running through it, and then only if it were held up to the sun. She hid the ring in her hand as a man and woman walked by the tent, the two of them speaking softly. When it was clear they were continuing on, Devorah slipped the ring on and concentrated. She felt for something, anything, that might indicate that the amethyst was one of Iri's Sacred Stones.

As the couple's footsteps faded, as their hushed words and the woman's giggles softened, she felt nothing. Nothing at all. She replaced the contents of the chest, including its false bottom, but kept the ring. She waited there for hours, holding it, trying ineffectually to convince herself that this was anything more than a normal jewel. Near dawn, she finally gave up. She wasn't sure if she was disappointed or not. It would be a wonder if it *had* been a fabled jewel like King Sukru had described, but who would wish for such a thing? Those tales always seemed to end in sorrow. Better, she thought, for the jewel to remain mundane, a bit of insurance should she and Leorah ever need it.

Just as the sun was rising, as she was lying down to sleep, Leorah rushed into the tent. Devorah debated whether to tell her, but she'd hidden the information thus far. Her mother had wished it so. *Don't tell her about the second ring,* Yael had said, *not yet. She's too wild. She'd only fritter it away. You're the responsible one. Sell it if need be, else keep it safely hidden.*

Devorah had done so, but just then, with Leorah standing over her, her expression of joy fading like stars at sunrise, she felt terrible for it.

"You won't even talk to me now?" Leorah asked as she flopped onto her bedding.

She thought Devorah was still angry about the race. "I'm only tired."

"You seemed awake enough when I came in."

"I'm tired, Leorah."

After a few moments of silence, Leorah came over and lay behind her. Devorah still wore the ring, but she'd turned it so that the jewel was resting in her palm, gripped by the fingers of her right hand.

"I'm sorry," Leorah whispered, "for everything. I know I should have spoken to you about the traverse first, but you'd only have tried to talk me out of it. That ring is *ours*. I won't let him have it."

Devorah nearly told her then. But instead, she hugged Leorah's arms more tightly around her and said, "I know."

They fell asleep like that, Leorah cradling Devorah, Devorah cradling the hidden amethyst.

As dawn broke on the third day following the end of the first contest, ten riders waited in a line, horses stamping and restless, their breath clouds that dissipated quickly in the cool morning air. Leorah sat on Wadi. All the horses seemed eager, but Wadi was full of nervous anticipation. He tugged at the reins, his tail swished, and the skin along his shoulders and flanks flicked.

To the right of the line, the winner's post no longer held ten pennants, but two, each representing one of the two riders who would move on to the third and final contest. Just beyond the post, Şelal held her whip at the ready. The morning celebration had just ended. Speeches had already been made.

The gathered crowd cheering her on, Şelal twice cracked her whip overhead. Like arrows from bows, Leorah and the other riders were off, heading toward Annam's Crook, the daunting black peak that loomed above them. The horses' hooves plodded onward, tails of sand kicking up behind, the sound like an approaching war party. As they rode further, the shallow dunes gave way to the earthy shelf below the mountain. The sound of their passing became sharper, their speed unfettered by the grasping sand.

Leorah had spent the past few days taking Wadi on easy rides to give the stallion a chance to recover but also to plan her ascent, which all riders were allowed, even encouraged, to do. There were three viable approaches, each with their own sets of challenges and advantages. The least taxing was an ascent along the mountain's western slope, but as the riders began this stage from the desert to the east, it was also the longest. The southeastern face was steep but also reasonably close, and for this reason, most riders took it. The last was the most difficult by far. The northeastern face. It was steep after the first few hours of riding, very steep, with many broken, knife-edge trails that could easily lead to injury for horse or rider or both. Only the most accomplished climbers dared take it, which meant that Kirhan was almost sure to opt for it.

When they approached the first fork in the trail, the swiftest horses, four of them, all from Tribe Okan, peeled away and rode hard along the easy terrain. Leorah and the five others, meanwhile, began the steeper climb toward the near side of the mountain. As she'd expected, Kirhan remained with her group.

Devorah hadn't shared everything about her conversation with Sukru, but she'd shared enough to make it clear just how important their mother's ring was to him; he would surely have made the price of failure clear to Kirhan, his champion. Not that Kirhan would need much urging. He was a gifted rider, a physical specimen, and, if rumor were true, an inspired climber.

But Leorah was no tent maiden, either. She'd always enjoyed climbing—the solitude, the crisp air, the vistas hidden from all save those who dared attack those heights. She might not be as strong as Kirhan, but he had a lot of weight to carry. She had the supple grace of a climber, and she vowed to cede no ground to him.

Wadi, as he'd been on the last part of the first contest, was like a horse reborn, and eager to match pace with Kirhan's gelding. As the two of them began outpacing the rest, Leorah got the impression they'd had this sort of race many times before. Indeed, as they approached the second split, Wadi drove even harder, tugging at the reins every time Leorah tried to slow his pace. Figuring he knew himself better than she did, she gave him all the reins he wanted. Wadi was healthy. Eager. He deserved a chance to win back his pride.

As they came to the split, Leorah was indecisive. She looked back. Saw Kirhan guiding his gelding toward the leftmost path, the one that would take him toward the easier southeastern face. She debated following, but realized a moment later, when she saw him crack a smile, that it was only a feint. She guided Wadi along the rightmost path, and Kirhan followed, laughing now, the sound of it rising above the rhythm of pounding hooves.

She hid her own smile by facing forward, crouching in her saddle as Wadi's pace devoured the expanse below the sharply climbing ground ahead. As she neared the mountain proper, she glanced over her shoulder and found that only Kirhan and Derya on her brass mare had joined her along the more dangerous route.

Derya was cause for worry. She was known as a consummate climber. She was thin as a blade, but strong, and she never wasted energy or effort, choosing her paths unerringly and with calm certainty.

On they went, attacking the incline, their speed slowing as the horses worked themselves into a lather. The land to either side of the path was littered with scrub brush, ironweed, and flowering bushes of purple and ivory and midnight blue.

To their left, in the distance, the first of the riders were passing around one long arm of the mountain. They'd be nearing a climb of their own in little time, but Leorah could spare them no mind. The trail was becoming rocky. The vegetation changed. Ironweed gave way to proper grasses. The bushes became taller evergreens. The path was still wide, but there were gaps here and there—all easily navigable, but they would grow worse. Much worse.

The air became cool and was a welcome relief to both Leorah and Wadi, who seemed to relish it, his head lifting high whenever a stiff breeze blew.

"Careful, now!" Kirhan called from fifty paces behind her. "Alir becomes skittish at the gaps."

Indeed, ahead was a place where the trail had given way to a dry rivulet. The slope went from steep on Leorah's right to a precipitous drop on her left. The valley was already dizzyingly far below them. Wadi stopped as he neared the gap. It was only as wide as Leorah's hips, but it was still far enough for an untrained horse, or one nervous of slides, to balk at.

Leorah stroked Wadi's neck and spoke softly, soothingly, "Kirhan's horse, the one *he* calls Alir, might have been afraid of this, but *you*, Wadi, are not. Wadi took to the desert and overcame the curse the gods placed on him. Wadi devoured the remainder of the race. Wadi forged a path up Annam's Crook while all others fell behind."

As she continued to stroke his bronze coat, Wadi stepped forward, shying toward the inclined side. His hooves slid, sending stones skittering down the slope, but then he was moving past.

"Good boy," Leorah said, her pride swelling. "None could have done better."

They continued, crossing larger and larger gaps. Wadi seemed to gain confidence with each one. Even so, he was not as bold as Kirhan's gelding or Derya's mare, and both of them soon used wider sections of the path to pass her by.

Near midday they finally reached the place where the horses would have to be left behind. Above was a sheer rock face they would need to navigate to reach the top. As in the desert race, three stood waiting at the top. They were at the edge of the cliff, staring down as the riders approached. The very fact that they were so interested gave Leorah hope that she, Kirhan, and Derya were the first to arrive.

After tying their horses to bushes, Kirhan and Derya began their ascent. Leorah, however, remained a moment. She studied the way up, looking for a path that might allow her to move ahead of the others. The other two, having arrived first, had already taken the obvious routes, the ones with many handholds and gaps in the rock, things they could use for surer traction, steadier progress.

Leorah found another path, one with easy footholds for a quarter of the distance up, and then a hairline crack that ran the rest of the way. Heart fluttering, she stared at it, envisioning her climb once, twice, while Kirhan and Derya both distanced themselves from her. Leorah was an able climber, but this was dangerous, almost foolhardy. Set aside the loss of the traverse and her mother's ring with it; a fall here could kill her.

But what was there to do? She needed to get ahead of one of them, Derya if not Kirhan.

Taking a deep breath, rubbing chalk over her hands from the bag at her back, she took to the climb. Up she went, quickly at first, then slowing her pace as she took more care to ensure her holds were secure and proper.

The right sort of leverage along the narrow crack in the rock face was crucial. Her fingers slipped into the cracks, holding as the soft leather soles of her boots found purchase. Her arms worked in concert with her shoulders, her back, her hips, her legs. Like an insect she climbed, steadily gaining on the other two, who had more winding climbs to assail than she did.

Her feet slipped only once. She'd been rushing, but she vowed renewed concentration, and gained the top just as Kirhan was pulling himself over the lip of the rock ledge to her left.

The two of them lumbered toward the post and slapped it almost simultaneously as, in the distance, along an easy slope to the east, four riders, the Black Wings of Tribe Okan, were hiking hard toward them. As Derya, breathing like an overworked bellows, reached the same post and slapped it, the Black Wings stared in wonder. They'd just realized they'd all likely lost. Only two could advance to the final contest; unless two or perhaps all three of the climbers that stood before them had some sort of accident on the way down, they'd have no chance of taking the long path back along the mountain's western face to reach the camp in time.

"Well done," said one, smiling, nodding his head to the impressive effort they'd put in so far. "I would already have fallen to my death," said another, a woman with a heart-shaped face and fearless eyes.

The Black Wings rested only a short while. As they jogged back along the easy eastern slope, Kirhan headed for the cliff. A short while later, so did Derya and Leorah. The downward climb was easier, but no less treacherous. It was difficult to see footholds. Their muscles were already near the point of failure, which only increased the need for care. Still, they all made good progress down.

And then disaster struck.

Kirhan had already reached level ground. Leorah was nearly there as well. But Derya slipped. She fell, scrabbling for an easy handhold a body length below her previous position. She missed this too and plummeted the last twenty feet. A sickening crunch obliterated the sounds of birds and buzzing insects. Derya rolled, releasing and endless scream while seizing one ankle.

Kirhan was on his gelding. He looked at Derya, then Leorah, who had just reached level ground. Brow furrowing, he pulled at his reins and gazed out across the great distance toward the camp, which could barely be discerned through the desert's amber haze, the many white tents and darker ships stippling the horizon. Even from this far away, King Sukru's galleon and pavilion could be seen, set apart from the gathered tribes.

As Leorah rushed to Derya's side, Kirhan kicked his silver akhala into a trot. Leorah ignored him, gasping when she saw Derya's ankle. Bone was sticking through. Derya was gripping her shin, just below her knee, her face white as she stared in horror at the wound.

As the sound of clopping hooves behind her faded, Leorah said, "All will be well," though it came out strained and forced. "All will be well," she said again, more confident this time, then rushed to Wadi's saddle bag, where each rider had bandages, splints, and various other remedies stored.

She gave Derya a small black blob of black lotus paste, placing it between her cheek and lower gum. "*Don't* swallow it," she said.

Derya's face was so grim Leorah wasn't sure she'd heard.

"Derya, *don't* swallow it! Do you hear me?"

Derya nodded, and then Leorah set to the work of straightening the bone. She wrapped bandages loosely around the wound, then placed the splints to either side of the break. Finally, she prepared the straps she would use to immobilize the broken bones.

"This will hurt," she said.

Derya, white-faced and sweating, nodded once, the gathered tears in her eyes shedding as she did so. "Just ruddy do it!"

Leorah pulled, and Derya screamed, louder than when she'd fallen, but her pain seemed to ease after that. Leorah worked quickly, tightening the straps, tightening the bandages, then wrapping more around the entire affair to help put pressure on the wound. It was imperfect. She was no physic to deal with a serious wound like this. But hopefully it was enough to see Derya down to the camp so she could be tended to properly.

"Drink," Leorah said, handing her a water skin. "All of it."

When Derya did, Leorah strapped another skin around her shoulders, then began the difficult business of getting Derya into her saddle. Working together, the two of them managed after a time. As Leorah mounted, the reality of the situation began to sink in. Long minutes had already passed. There would be no winning this traverse now. Not with Kirhan so far ahead. Surely at least one and possibly several of the other riders would be approaching the fork where this trail met the others.

Behind her, Derya groaned. Leorah turned to see her eyes fluttering, slipping forward in her saddle.

"Oh, gods!" She pulled Wadi's reins sharply over and managed to catch Derya just as she was slipping sideways off her saddle. She muscled Derya's limp form across Wadi's rump, wondering now if she'd make it down the mountain in time to save Derya's life.

Guiding Wadi with in one hand, she used her other to both keep Derya firmly in place and grip the reins of her horse. Like this, they made their way down the mountain. But then they reached the first of the gaps in the trail. She could see the hoof marks they'd left on the way up. She could see the marks from Kirhan's gelding as it had headed down. Wadi, skittish earlier, refused to cross the gap.

"Come on, boy," Leorah said as soothingly as she could manage, which to her own ear was not soothing at all. "This is nothing. Simpler than the way up!"

Wadi, however, would not be convinced. He refused to go any further no matter what she tried. The trail was too thin to try to get Derya back onto her own akhala. She'd likely lose Derya's horse or Wadi or both to the steep slope. Even a small slide at this point would likely be a death sentence for Derya.

She splashed water on Derya's face, hoping to wake her, to have her help. She tried to convince Wadi to go. She even leaned forward and tried to feed him a dried pear, hoping the familiarity might calm his nerves, but Wadi would only roll his eyes and neigh and jerk his head away each time she tried. He became so frantic he nearly lost his footing. Stones and earth skittered down the mountainside to her right. Wadi managed to recover, but the scare seemed to have scraped his nerves raw.

He stamped, shying away from the gap, in the process butting into Derya's mare, which was also becoming nervous. The mare, feeding off Wadi's nervous energy, jerked her head back, then reared and struck Wadi's rump with her forehooves when he'd backed into her one too many times.

Wadi jumped forward several steps, screaming from the pain, then halted at the very edge of the gap. His tail swished wildly. The skin along his shoulders and rump flicked constantly.

Leorah was starting to lose her hold on Derya. "Please, Wadi! Please calm down!"

But Wadi wouldn't listen. He continued to scream, to try to back away, but Derya's mare refused to give ground. The constant stamping was causing the ground beneath him to crumble. More and more rocks were sliding and skittering down the mountainside.

Leorah was just preparing to drop down to try to calm Wadi when she heard a high whistle. It rose in pitch, then stopped. It came again a moment later, birdlike—a long note followed by a high-pitched whoop.

Wadi visibly calmed. His stamping slowed. He was no longer screaming, but instead seemed to be listening, trying to determine where the sound had come from.

Around a bend far ahead came Kirhan on his silver gelding, the forefinger and thumb of one hand pinched between his teeth. Again the whistle came.

Now that Wadi could see him, his nerves settled further. Then his nervous motions vanished altogether. His eyes no longer rolled. His breathing was strong but steady.

As Kirhan rode closer, Leorah realized how chagrined he looked. "I should have told you, he's worse going down."

"So I've learned." Part of her wanted to feel angry at him for abandoning them, but in truth, she felt only relief.

Kirhan dropped down and crossed the gap. He guided Wadi over it, stroking his muzzle, whispering softly, while Leorah held Derya tightly. Soon they'd made it across, and the three of them were riding down slowly but steadily. Each time they came to another gap, Kirhan dropped from his saddle, guided Wadi over it, then remounted. Wadi eventually regained some courage and began traversing the gaps tentatively on his own.

It felt like a divine miracle when they finally reached more level ground. Deepening the feeling was the fact that Derya soon woke. "Stop," she said with an uncharitable look at both Leorah and Kirhan. "Stop it! Stop moving! This bloody fucking hurts!"

Leorah laughed nervously. So did Kirhan.

With Leorah's help, Derya managed to make it to a seated position behind Leorah. Her face was doughy and white, but miraculously, she seemed alert and ready to ride.

They moved with some speed after that. Down they went, finally nearing the fork in the trail. Ahead, two riders approached from the southeastern pass, riding hard. Leorah had no idea if they were the first to come this way or not, but what did it matter? She couldn't manage a racing pace. Not with Derya behind her.

The riders passed them as they reached the fork and headed for camp: long-limbed Urdman and his son, Ornük. They looked to Derya with concern on their faces and pulled up.

"Can we help?" Urdman asked.

"No," Leorah said. "Go on."

They nodded, then urged their horses back into a gallop.

"You go as well," Derya said.

Leorah turned in her saddle. "Don't be foolish."

"Go," she said, taking her mare's reins from the horn of Leorah's saddle. "I won't have either of you losing the race because of me."

Leorah was about to deny her, but Derya was already using the reins to draw her mare beside her. She leaned forward and then, with an almighty grunt that accompanied her inelegant movements, she swung herself over to the mare's saddle. The sounds Derya made were filled with cursing and clear pain, but when she'd settled herself again, she looked as if she could keep her saddle as long as she went slowly.

"Go." She motioned to the path behind where in the distance another rider was coming into view. "Others will be along soon if I need help."

Kirhan stared at Leorah, a questioning look.

Leorah shrugged, then nodded.

And then the two of them were off, racing, the hooves of their horses barely seeming to touch the dry ground as they powered onward.

They caught up to Urdman and Ornük, passed them by as they were nearing the last fork, the one that led to the mountain's western face. Only then did they see that there was another rider ahead, the Black Wing who'd congratulated them at the top of the mountain.

Leorah had no idea if he was the only one ahead, but she refused to give in until she knew the race was lost. Kirhan was the same. The camp ahead came into sharper view. They closed the distance steadily. The Black Wing was a quarter-league ahead, then an eighth-league. Then he was only a stone's throw away and looking over his shoulder at them with wide, nervous eyes.

By now the three of them were nearing the edge of camp. As they reached the sand, the crowd was cheering. Amber tails kicked up behind them as they galloped hard for the finish line.

Leorah saw Şelal. She saw Sukru.

Most importantly, she saw Devorah, standing alone, hands clasped beneath her chin. *I'm so sorry for what I've done,* Leorah thought as she concentrated on the way ahead. *I'll make you proud. I promise. And then I'll make it up to you.*

As they neared the finish line, both she and Kirhan edged past the Black Wing. Kirhan crossed first, Leorah second. As the cheers of the crowd shook the desert, the two lone pennants were taken down.

The entrants to the final contest had now been set.

Devorah watched from afar as the celebration for the traverse's second contest was winding down. Leorah and Kirhan were drinking together, telling tales by the fire with many of the other riders, including Derya, who lay nearby, her broken leg propped up as she sipped from a flask the physic had given her. It was a restorative, but it seemed to be making her just as drunk as the rest of the gathering.

Devorah wanted to speak to Leorah—about all that had happened in Sukru's tent, about the amethyst's supposed abilities, about the second ring—but she wasn't ready for that. Not yet. There were more questions that needed answering first. So while it might not have been the perfect time to speak with Leorah, it did seem the perfect time to find some of those answers.

Everyone was occupied with someone, including Şelal and Armesh, who were busy speaking with the other shaikhs, and would be for some time.

When a new song was picked up by a rebab, a lay of Bahri Al'sir, a pair of flutes and a dozen drums joined in, and all those around the fires lifted their voices in song. Devorah took the opportunity to lose herself in the darkness. She'd not gone a dozen steps, however, when a hand landed on her shoulder.

She turned to find Leorah standing there, looking confused, perhaps hurt. "Where are you going?"

Devorah held herself around the middle, made herself small as she motioned to the gathering behind her. "It's very loud."

"It's a celebration," Leorah said, "for *my* victory."

"I know, but the noise. It's creeping into my bones. I'm starting to itch from it."

Leorah looked crestfallen, like she had when they were children. She was so used to getting into trouble she'd always expected extra helpings of praise when she managed to do something to be proud of. "Aren't you happy for me?"

Devorah realized how unkind she was being. What Leorah had done *was* an incredible accomplishment.

She took Leorah into her arms. "Of course I'm

happy for you. What you did today I could never have done, not in a thousand years."

Leorah hugged her back, then pulled away. "Then *join* us! Come sit by the fire and sing!"

Devorah shook her head. "It really is too much for me. But we'll celebrate another time, yes? We'll go into the desert and share hummus and olives and flatbread, like we used to."

Leorah opened her mouth to object, but then stopped herself. She nodded once, smiling. "I'd like that." After placing a quick kiss on Devorah's cheek, she was back at the fire, sitting by Kirhan's side, nuzzling into him and raising her glass of silver araq as they hit the refrain.

Devorah left and wandered between the tents. When she was certain she wasn't being followed, she went to the largest: Şelal's. A guard was posted, but it was only Old Khyrn, who hated revels just as much as Devorah did. He was sitting in a folding chair, slumped—awake, but close to nodding off.

Devorah slipped around the back of the tent, undid two of the lower ties, and slipped under the canvas. She crept across the carpets, looking through various boxes. She found what she was looking for a short while later. Sukru's chest of golden rahl was set beside Şelal's larger chest of clothes. Behind it was the prize offered by Tribe Okan, the Sword of the Willow. It was leaning against an old, beaten chest. The chest had no lock on it—this race was too sacred, the prizes too recognizable, for thievery to be a concern. Devorah opened the chest to find the golden chalice of Bahri Al'sir, and her mother's second ring.

She pulled the ring's twin from the pouch at her belt and by the light of the moons filtering in through the roof compared them. They were nearly identical—rings no doubt crafted by the same jeweler.

Staring at them, she was disappointed. She wasn't sure what she could have expected, though. For their secrets to unfold like night-blooming roses? She slipped the cracked one onto her left hand, the other onto her right. She closed her eyes, as she had with the one her mother had given her in secret. She *felt* for… she knew not what. The warmth in the air, the night breeze filtering in through the gaps at the base of the tent's walls. She heard songs being sung, the thrum of conversation. She felt the weight of both rings. But beyond this. Nothing.

Until she neared the tent flaps.

From the ring on her right hand she sensed something deeper than the cool night air, something deeper than the desert. Like the creeping feeling when someone approaches from behind, it was a thing unseen yet clearly present, subtle as the scent of jasmine at spring's failing. The more she concentrated on it, though, the more distinct it became. Khyrn, she realized, as remote as the moons only a moment ago, now felt nearer to her. Not in any physical sense. No, he felt like a memory, insubstantial and yet no less real for it, growing brighter the more she thought on it. She almost felt as if she could speak to him.

She had half a mind to try when she felt another presence nearing. A moment later she heard footsteps. The fear that she might be discovered spiked as a voice huffed in irritation. "Why do we allow you to do anything?"

Armesh's voice, a soft rebuke for how easily Khyrn found his slumber these days.

Devorah rushed toward the chest to replace the ring, but too late. The ties of the tent flap were pulled aside and Armesh stepped in. Devorah spun, hiding her hands behind her back, but Armesh had already seen. Even if he hadn't, it wouldn't take a collegia master to guess why she'd stolen into the tent.

Armesh stepped outside. A soft cry of surprise from Khyrn followed. "I've returned," Armesh said softly.

"You may go."

Khyrn's chair creaked. She heard him brushing down his clothes, clearing his throat a moment later. "As you wish."

As his footsteps faded, Armesh stepped back inside, lit a lamp, then regarded Devorah steadily. "The ring," he said, holding one palm out to her.

She removed the dead one behind her back and placed it in his palm. He frowned, then held it back out for her to take. "Not the dead one."

Devorah stared, shocked, confused, her mind fighting to craft some combination of words that would allow her to keep the other ring.

But Armesh was already growing impatient. He flicked the fingers of his other hand. "The ring, Devorah. The prize promised to the winner of the traverse."

Feeling small as a child before a scolding grandparent, Devorah pulled it off her hand and held it out, accepting the other ring back from him.

"You know your mother and I were close." He held the ring up and stared into the facets of the amethyst, which glittered in the lantern's light like the flames of a distant bonfire. "You may not realize *how* close, however. I taught her how to ride her first horse. She taught me my letters when my mother refused to. I stole her first kiss just days after she'd been chosen for your father. Did she ever tell you?" Lowering the ring, he regarded her with a wistful look. "No, I suppose she wouldn't have."

"What do you know about that ring, Armesh? Why does Sukru want it?"

"Why would a King of Sharakhai want *anything* of power? To keep it from the tribes, I suppose. To steal away yet more of our heritage and hide it in the bowels of their palaces."

"There must be more. He's *obsessed* with it." She told him of her meal with King Sukru, especially how hungry he'd become when speaking of the ring. "I could hear it in the way he asked his questions. I saw it in his eyes. He knows what it can do. He just doesn't know *how*." She paused, waiting for him to answer her unspoken question. When he didn't, she said, "Do *you*, Armesh? Do you know how it's used?"

He waggled his head, his curly grey hair waving along his shoulders. "What does it matter? It will soon be Sukru's."

Devorah frowned. "Leorah might yet win." It was an unreasonable hope, and they both knew it.

"The traverse was always going to come down to

Kirhan and one other contestant. It just happens to be your sister. The final outcome has never been, and still is not, in doubt."

"How does the gemstone work?" Devorah pressed.

"Listen to me now. It doesn't *matter.* This one is lost, and the other is broken. You'll have no chance to use it."

"How do you know one is broken?"

He looked at her incredulously. "Do you think you're the only one who can sneak into a tent and open a chest? I made a *point* of knowing, Devorah."

She held the flawed ring aloft. "If you ever loved my mother, you'll tell me. You'll let me replace that ring with this one and you'll tell me what it does."

"I promised your mother I'd keep you safe. What you suggest is the perfect opposite of that."

"Armesh, *tell* me!"

At this, he only stared at her sadly, as if she were a waif he'd found stumbling in the desert. "I care for you, Devorah. You and Leorah, both. Which is why I will do no such thing." He moved to the tent flap and pulled it back. "Now go. And by the gods, show that ring to no one, least of all Leorah."

She wanted to rage, wanted to beat him with her fists like Leorah would certainly do, but he would not relent—she could see it in his sandstone expression—so she left without another word.

As the festivities began to wind down, Leorah gave one last look to Kirhan, who was sitting with a throng of revelers, regaling them with tales of Sharakhai, then she made for the tent set aside for the two champions.

In truth she didn't want this night to end—with the morning came the all-too-real possibility that her quest to win back her mother's ring would come to a crashing halt—but she needed sleep if she were to have any chance of winning.

Ducking inside the tent, she stumbled, only then realizing how wobbly she was. She shouldn't have drunk so much. Kirhan had hardly touched his araq. He'd swallowed enough to avoid giving offense, but she'd seen him time and time again nursing his drink.

Always the thick-headed mule, Leorah.

Her own revelry could have waited one more day. It was just that she'd been so relieved Derya hadn't died. And even after her survival seemed assured, Leorah had thought surely others would win the final two pennants. When she'd taken the second, a great joy had bubbled up inside her, a feeling so strong she hadn't wanted it to end.

After guzzling water from the ewer that had been left for her, she lay down and listened to the hum of conversation, the crackling of the fire. She woke some time later to the sounds of someone entering the tent. Limned in moonlight, Kirhan's broad form stepped inside and closed the flap behind him. He moved to his blankets and sat down, cross-legged. She couldn't tell what he was doing for a moment. His silhouette was distorting strangely. And then she realized.

"By the gods, you're *stretching*?"

He paused. "Drink tightens the muscles."

Leorah sat up and faced him. "You're limber enough."

"*You* may think so."

She wished she had some biting reply, but as calm as he made her feel she probably wouldn't have voiced it anyway. "Thank you for coming back for us."

She saw him shake his head, the barest of movements in the darkness. "I deserve no thanks. The gods will judge me harshly for having left you."

"You came back. That's what's important."

"Don't pour honey on my shame, Leorah Mikel'ava.

I was a coward."

She paused. She hadn't realized he knew her full name. "Wanting to win the traverse is hardly cowardice."

It took him a long time to respond. "You don't understand."

"Then help me to."

Outside, a woman giggled, then screamed in mirth as someone chased her about the dying fire. "It's Sukru," Kirhan finally said. "He wants the amethyst."

"It was a difficult puzzle to solve, but I'd somehow worked that part out."

She'd hoped he would laugh, but he didn't. In a voice as serious as she'd ever heard him use, he said, "You don't know the half of it. He's been searching for that gem for many years. You understand me? *Many* years."

A chill began to creep along Leorah's arms, making the hair stand up. "What are you saying?"

"I've heard the tales of the attack on Tribe Tulogal, the one that saw your parents and brother dead. It wasn't a simple clash over the new shipping tariffs the Kings imposed, as most now claim. It was an excuse for Sukru to attack your tribe so that he might find the amethyst."

The chill along her arms crept inside her chest. "*Sukru* sent them?"

In the darkness, Kirhan nodded. "An informant was paid handsomely for the information. He knew the amethyst was there. He was nearly certain your family had it hidden away somewhere. He'd hoped to take it quickly, by force, and hide the knowledge that it had ever existed. Your parents were killed. Your brother as well. But you and your sister were spirited away. Sukru never learned how, but he's been searching for you ever since."

Leorah folded her arms around her waist, a vain attempt at suppressing the trembling that had broken out all over her body. "*That's* why he's come?"

"Yes. He learned of the amethyst and asked Şelal to deliver it to him. She's a prideful woman, though. She felt honor bound not to deliver it to him outright, lest she appear craven to her own tribe, or worse, the neighboring tribes. She arranged for the ring to be one of the prizes of the traverse, a way for Sukru to obtain it without Şelal being blamed of any wrongdoing."

"And then Sukru came to you." Kirhan was a man selected from hundreds, surely, perhaps thousands. He was a champion, a man who wouldn't be denied this prize.

"Yes," he said, "and I will not step aside. My *family* is in Sharakhai. All of them—my grandmother, my uncles and aunts, my cousins—are beholden to Sukru."

"Your mother and father?"

"My mother died in childbirth along with my baby sister. My father some years later. A fall from the vulture's nest of a caravan ship."

"I'm sorry."

A pause. "It happened a long time ago."

One last whoop came from the woman being chased outside, and then there was silence, the sounds of low whispers.

"I didn't ask you to step aside," Leorah said.

"I know. You're a prideful woman. You'd never ask for it, nor even wish for it. But I wish to be clear with you. In the morning, I will take the prize. It would be better for you and your sister, I think, if you just let me."

"If you think *I* will step aside, you're mad."

Kirhan lay down. Faced away from her. "Think on it, Leorah. You've much to live for. Let this bauble go."

Leorah lay down as well. She curled into a ball, wishing her family was still with her, wishing the amethyst had never entered their lives. Most of all, a flame was melting the cold that had gathered inside her, burning it away like the sun in the depths of desert's winter.

She had a mind to go to Sukru's ship and kill him, regardless of what happened to her. If she did, though, if she even tried, Devorah would suffer for it, perhaps only *after* being taken back to Sharakhai and tortured. Others in the tribe would also be punished. Şelal would likely be put to death. Perhaps Armesh as well, as a warning for all who would harbor assassins against the Kings.

She couldn't do it. She couldn't put Devorah and others in that sort of peril. The ring, however, was another matter entirely.

That she could take. *That* she could win away, even as Sukru's grasping, claw-like fingers reached for it. She would do it, she decided. She felt for Kirhan and for his family in Sharakhai—he was a victim here as well—but she refused to let that cloud her thoughts. The ring was hers, hers and Devorah's, and she would win it back, Sukru and his champion be damned.

She lay awake a long while, unable to sleep. In the end, it was imagining the look on Sukru's face that allowed her to find her way into the land of sleep.

As the sun glared over the eastern mountains, Leorah sat in Wadi's saddle wearing leather-and-chain armor. Her conical helm had a filigreed nose guard, a tall spike atop, and a curtain of chainmail that lapped at her shoulders. Her left arm, the same one that gripped Wadi's reins, was fitted through the straps of a shield. A coiled whip was held in the other.

A hundred paces distant was Kirhan, sitting atop his silver akhala. He was similarly armored. The wind toyed with the egret plumes sweeping back from his helm. His shield glinted brightly in the sun. He looked like a hero of old, a man preparing to lead an army to war. His spear had a straight blade and hook on one end, a blunt club on the other. It was short—a spear made for close combat, a good choice to knock an opponent from her saddle.

All around them, in a grand circle, were the people of the three gathered tribes, as well as those who had accompanied Sukru to the desert: the crew of his galleon, some few advisors, and servants. To one side, along Leorah's left, a pavilion had been erected. Its roof flapped in the stiff morning wind. Şelal sat within, as did the stout Shaikh Duyal of Okan and the long-limbed Jherrok of Narazid. Sukru was there as well, crook-backed in his chair, watching with pinched eyes, hands clasped before him, a ravenous man moments before the feast. His two Blade Maidens stood behind him, stoic, watching.

The urge in Leorah was strong to charge Sukru and cut him with her whip, to strike for his neck and see him bleed. The Maidens may protect him, the *gods* may protect him, but that didn't mean they could protect him from all things. She wished to see fear in his eyes. She wished to see him run from her before she rode him down with Wadi's sharp hooves.

The spell was broken when Şelal made her way into the sun. All was silence. All were rapt as she lifted one hand.

"Two remain in the traverse. To the winner goes the spoils, and yet these are small compared to the glory the victor will take with them to the farther fields." She lifted her hand higher. "Go well, champions. May the light of the gods shine upon you!"

When Şelal dropped her hand, the voices of the crowd lifted higher than they'd ever been, even at the finish line of the second contest. Kirhan kicked his horse into a gallop. Leorah did the same. As she leaned into the rhythm of Wadi's accelerating pace, she allowed her whip to uncoil. It trailed behind, a writhing snake skipping over the sand.

As Kirhan came nearer, he lowered his spear, pointed it over Wadi's head, directly at Leorah's chest. Leorah tightened her legs on Wadi's barrel chest. She hunkered low and raised her shield. Kirhan looked so menacing in his armor she nearly abandoned her plan and struck with the whip early. But she stayed her hand and waited. She was only going to have one chance at this.

Her body fell in tune with Wadi's gait. She watched the tip of Kirhan's spear warily, waiting for any small shift. At the last possible moment, he lifted it up and in a blinding arc swung the blunt end into her path. He was hoping to bash her from her saddle. Leorah was ready, however. She leaned even lower, guessing, correctly, that he would wish no harm to come to Wadi.

The spear's blunt weight crashed against her shield. It struck like a battering ram despite her trying to angle the weight up and away. She was nearly flipped from her saddle. But she held.

And now it's my turn.

With a grunt and a sharp twist of her upper body, she sent her whip flying. Kirhan was nearly out of reach already, so fast were their horses galloping over the sand, but the spear's lance still trailed behind him.

The whip caught it just below the hooked head. Gripping Wadi's chest and the whip as hard as she could, she yanked on it.

She felt a tug, then nothing.

The crowd gasped as the spear twisted up and away from Kirhan's grip. It flipped into the air, the whip coming free of the haft as it spun. The way the sun caught the blade's gleaming edge made it look like a weapon forged by Thaash himself.

Even before it landed, Kirhan was pulling on the reins of his horse. He *needed* that weapon.

But Leorah was ready. She pulled on Wadi's reins as well. Wadi halted and spun, eager and excited now that the battle had begun. She charged forward as Kirhan leaned precariously in his saddle. He was gripping the saddle horn with one hand, his left leg hooked over his horse's rear, just behind the saddle. She hadn't really appreciated it until now, but his wingspan was incredible. Hanging low, his right hand hovered just above the sand. In only a few moments, his horse's long strides would deliver to him his spear.

Leorah sent her whip cracking, once, twice, three times, as Kirhan approached the fallen spear. The first two were warnings. The third, when she realized he wasn't going to back off, aimed for his reaching hand.

It caught him across the wrist, to stunning effect. Bits of flesh flew from the point of impact while blood coursed from the wound, coating his hand.

Miraculously, he *still* almost managed to take up the spear, but it slipped between his fingers as he was trying to lift himself back up to the saddle. The crowd gasped as his foot suddenly dropped from the stirrup and both feet dragged across the ground, but his left hand still gripped the saddle horn.

Leorah tried to take advantage. She sent the whip at his legs, hoping to grab an ankle and yank him free of his horse. The whip's end spun around his shin, but he immediately squirmed his leg free. Guessing she might try again, he let out a series of short, sharp whistles, and his horse spun, effectively fouling her aim.

She couldn't let the opportunity go, though. She couldn't let him recover. She urged Wadi into a charge, shot her whip forward as Kirhan's head lifted up from the opposite side of his saddle. He still had his shield, and used it to block a pair of stinging strikes. By then the two horses were too close for her to try again.

He was hiding his right hand, she realized. Concealing something. Still, she didn't expect him to swing a bloody great iron hook toward her.

The weapon was about the length of a riding crop.

It could certainly do damage if he managed to land a blow, but the real danger was him hooking her armor and pulling her from her saddle.

She blocked his initial swing, but he tried again and again, changing up the angle and power each time. On the fourth swing, she felt it catch along her right side.

He immediately guided his akhala away and began pulling at the hook mercilessly.

The horses were facing in opposite directions. Leorah grabbed her saddle tightly and tried to rein Wadi over to move in the same direction as Kirhan's horse. But his horse was already plowing forward with gathering speed, and Wadi couldn't keep up.

Seeing the end drawing near, Leorah grew desperate. She swung her whip in a low arc, behind his horse's rump. It swung lazily around the horse's back hocks, then snapped around its fetlocks. She pulled hard. For a moment she thought the whip hadn't held, but it was only the slack in the whip being drawn up. A moment later it cinched tight around the horse's legs. Hopes soaring, she reached forward and pulled again, straining as hard as she could.

Kirhan's horses were trained for war, but that mattered little here. Having its legs trapped couldn't help but spook even a well seasoned warhorse. It neighed and stumbled, eyes rolling. Hobbled as it was, it moved *toward* Leorah. It also bucked and kicked, once catching Wadi across the shoulder, but Wadi stood strong, fearless.

One last time Leorah grabbed for the slack and yanked, grunting hard as the whip's leather creaked. To her surprise, Kirhan tossed his shield aside. With his right hand still gripping the hook, he used his off hand to draw the knife at his belt, preparing to cut the whip.

That was when his horse suddenly reared.

The silver akhala's dark legs clawed skyward. It was a foolish thing to do, wrapped up as it was, but the beast couldn't possibly understand the situation. It was desperate. It tried to balance itself, hopped backward several times, then began to tip over.

Kirhan, eyes wide, dropped the knife and grabbed for his saddle, but still held tight to the gods-damned hook. Leorah was going to go down with him, she realized, and then it was anyone's guess as to who would win. Whoever struck the earth last, she supposed. So she did the only thing she could think of. She released the whip, crouched on her saddle, and leapt *toward* Kirhan.

Kirhan tried using the hook to pull her beyond

his horse, forcing her loss, but she anticipated it and kept her body low. She landed awkwardly, straddling his horse's belly as it went down along its right side. Kirhan, however, was trapped. The horse fell hard on his right leg.

He screamed, finally, blessedly releasing the hook.

The whip was still tight, but it loosened as his horse kicked. It was trying to right itself. Kirhan was trying to follow it up, using the reins to stay on. Indeed, he may yet win the contest. Leorah was scrabbling to remain on his horse; she was situated so strangely she might be thrown at any moment.

But Kirhan was in a bad way. He could hardly prevent her from what she did next.

Pulling her own knife, she balanced on the horse's belly and back, ready for the horse to roll onto its legs. When the horse lifted, she cut the reins Kirhan was using to steady himself and shoved him hard to one side.

Over he tipped, while Leorah lunged forward and grabbed two fistfuls of the horse's dark mane.

Kirhan fell to the sand with a hard thump, groaning as he gripped his right leg, which had surely been broken.

Incredibly, she kept hold of the gelding's mane and somehow managed to land in the saddle. The silver akhala was skittish, running and kicking strangely for a moment, but then at last it settled.

That was when the cheering of the crowd came to her. All in a rush she heard them, thousands of people cheering the tribeswoman who'd bested the champion of a King of Sharakhai. Their hands were up. Their voices rang to the sky, rang to the heavens.

From the pavilion, Şelal watched with open-mouthed shock. Sukru, meanwhile, merely stared. He took in the crowd, then Şelal, and finally Leorah, with a withering glare, as if he were thinking of uncoiling his own fabled whip and using it to loose Leorah's head from her shoulders, let her body fall on the sand beside Kirhan's writhing form.

But then a calm seemed to overcome him. He shared with her a knowing smile, then strode from the field like a peacock.

Devorah watched with bated breath as Kirhan fell. By the gods, Leorah had won. Leorah had *won*!

Relief flooded through her.

But Leorah seemed anything but relieved. Devorah followed her gaze and saw the look Sukru was giving her: cold as the dawn, deadly as nightshade. When he turned and strode from the pavilion, Devorah's nervousness increased. The crowd rushed forward to congratulate the two combatants and to tend to Kirhan's injury.

A stretcher was brought. Kirhan was rushed away to the King's physic to be tended to. The festivities, meanwhile, had already begun. Leorah was greeted by many. So many that Devorah hardly dared approach her. This was a time of happiness. She should let Leorah have it. Devorah would only poison Leorah's joy with her worries.

It was for this reason, after a time of seeing her dance with the most enthusiastic of the revelers—all of them from Tribe Rafik—that Devorah walked away. Just as she was reaching the edge of camp, she heard someone behind her calling, "Wait!" She turned to find Leorah running toward her. "Wait! Where are you going?"

What could she say? She motioned half-heartedly toward the tents where everyone was gathering for the feast. "You'll have much to attend to."

"Much to *attend* to?" She lifted her right hand, where the amethyst glittered brightly. "Devorah, I *won* memma's ring back! It's time to celebrate!"

"Yes," Devorah said. "Of course."

"Yes," Leorah said with a pouty expression, *"of course.* Devorah, this is grand! We've won, and *you* are going to celebrate with me."

And they did. They drank. They sang. Even Devorah, despite her misgivings. Leorah was anxious about Kirhan, so much so that when he was carried on a chair to the edge of the fire, she went to him, dropped to her knees, and spoke to him for a long while. Now and again, Kirhan would motion to the bandages and splint that had immobilized his leg from the thigh all the way down to his ankle. Leorah listened to it all, her eyes bright as a newborn foal's.

It had been many years since Devorah had seen Leorah smitten. Truly smitten. She was ashamed to admit that there was a twinge of jealousy it wasn't *her* sitting by Kirhan's side, but she was happy for her sister.

Strangely absent from the proceedings was Şelal. Sukru was missing as well, but that only made sense. The loss surely stung. Near nightfall, after a feast that had lasted the entire day, Şelal returned. She wore a beautiful blue dress, a jalabiya that accented her eyes, her jeweled earrings, and the thread-of-gold turban she wore atop her head. Her expression was one of forced joy. Devorah could see thoughts warring within her, even before she went near the largest of the fires and waved for all to attend her.

"We come at last to the end!"

A great roar shook the sands of the desert.

She motioned to Leorah with a bow of her head. "And we have our champion!"

Leorah beamed, and the roar grew louder still, especially from the women, who shouted in joy, "Lai, lai, lai, lai!" Devorah, however, was growing ever more nervous. Şelal was building up to something.

"The traverse ends tomorrow. So we take to the sands once more. We thank Jherrok and Duyal and their tribes for joining us here. We thank the Kings of Sharakhai, who sent one of their own to join in the celebration of this race." She motioned to Leorah, but refused to look at her. "I am proud of our champion. Proud that she persevered, that she helped Derya Redknife to return to us, that she displayed such skill against a man with so storied a life it matches even the men of old. I will be proud to see her represent Tribe Rafik in Sharakhai."

The commotion around the fire rumbled to an awkward silence, then died altogether. Some had not heard clearly. A susurrus of conversation built at the edges of the gathering as some tried to clarify what

Şelal had just said.

Devorah had heard every word. And her heart was now pounding in her ears.

The smile on Şelal's face was half-hearted at best. It was the regret behind her eyes, however, that worried Devorah the most. "I have the pleasure to announce to all that King Sukru, after seeing how masterfully one of our own has conducted herself, has decided to take a bride."

The shout in Devorah's throat was burning, building, even before Şelal had finished. *"Noooo! Noooooooo!"*

Şelal went on, louder, as if she hadn't heard. "On the morrow, Leorah Mikel'ava al Rafik will accompany King Sukru to the Desert's Amber Jewel, where they will be married before the whole of Sharakhai."

Devorah found herself walking, then marching, then sprinting headlong toward Şelal until someone grabbed her arm. She stumbled. Yanked her arm away and kept moving. A half-dozen now stood in her path, barring her, pressing her back. "No! He cannot have her!"

Şelal stared at Leorah with a forlorn look—a look of regret, Devorah supposed it was meant to seem—while Leorah stared in silence at the bright horizon. Disbelief filled her eyes. Shock. Devorah had never seen her sister look so lost.

"He may have the ring! Tell him he may have the ring!"

At last, Şelal regarded her. "This is no longer about the ring."

"He cannot have my sister!"

The look Şelal gave her was one of pity half hidden behind the stony facade of a shaikh. "It is already decided," she said, then turned and walked away.

There were those who seemed angry, those who seemed shocked and disappointed, but no one made a move to help her. No one lifted their voice to forestall what amounted to theft—theft of the treasures of the traverse, which would now be given to Sukru as part of his bride price; the theft of a woman who'd done harm to no one, who'd helped Tribe Rafik since the day they had accepted her.

"Is it because she's an outsider?"

At last Leorah turned, her eyes wide. "Devorah, be quiet."

But Devorah went on. She would say these words, force Şelal to respond to them. If she didn't, she would always regret it. "Is it because she's not one of your own?"

Leorah was now sprinting toward her. "Be *quiet*,"

she hissed, and pressed Devorah away from the crowd, away from the fire, away from the other tribes and the few of Sukru's crewmen who'd come to the celebration, who might at any moment relay Devorah's words back to their King.

"You'll get us both killed," Leorah said when they'd moved deeper into the Rafik camp, out of earshot. "It's done, Devorah."

Two warm trails of tears burned their way down Devorah's cheeks. "I won't let him take you."

"It's too late. If I deny him, he'll kill *me*. If I run, he'll kill *you*."

"We can *both* run, as we did before!"

Leorah gripped her arms tightly. "He'll be expecting it, Devorah."

"I won't be parted from you."

"He won't allow you to join me." Her eyes drifted to the masts of Sukru's galleon, visible over the nearby tents. "It would give me too much joy."

Now it was Devorah's turn to grip Leorah's arms. "I *won't* be parted from you."

Leorah was crying freely now. "I'm so sorry I did this, Devorah. You were right. It was selfish of me."

Hearing footsteps approaching, Devorah swallowed her reply. From around the corner of a nearby tent, Şelal appeared and strode toward them. She came to a stop several paces away and motioned to Leorah's hand. "Sukru has asked that the prizes be brought to him."

Leorah blinked. She lifted her hand and stared at the ring. "He can't have it. It's mine."

"Don't make this difficult. It *is* his. *You* are his."

Leorah spit on the sand between them. "He may force our marriage, but I will *never* be his."

"How could you have done this," Devorah broke in, "sold Leorah away like a common mule?"

Şelal turned her head with an imperious air, a thing Devorah wanted to slap from her face. "What I did I did for the good of the tribe *and* the two of you. Leorah was foolish to have entered the traverse. She was foolish to have won it. Better to have let the ring go from the beginning. I don't know how Sukru learned of it, but once he had, he meant to have it. And now he will."

"You *offered* it to him," Leorah said.

Surprise showed on Şelal's face, but she recovered quickly. "He'd already learned that it had come here. I offered it to protect Tribe Rafik. I couldn't have him thinking I was trying to hide it from him."

"Coward," Leorah spat.

"You may think so, but try wearing the turban of a shaikh for a year. Keeping a tribe alive is difficult enough. Worse when the Kings turn their eyes on you, ready to drain you of blood whenever it pleases them. They did it to my father. They did it to my grandfather. I won't let it happen again. Sukru is one of the pettiest among them. He has killed for less than hiding baubles." She held out the palm of her hand like a disapproving grandmother. "Now give me the ring, Leorah."

"I'm not married to him yet," Leorah said.

Şelal was clearly exasperated, tired of fighting, yet her hand remained where it was. "Don't be a child. You know how this must go."

But before Devorah or Leorah could respond, a man's voice cut in. "It is not yet his. Even Sukru cannot deny it." It was Armesh. He was ambling toward them, hands clasped behind his back. "Tell him she wishes to hold it for the night. This one night only. And that when they depart for Sharakhai in the morning, he may have it."

Şelal hesitated, unsure of herself.

"Or if you cannot summon the courage to tell him, I will, though I don't think he'll take it kindly from me."

"He won't take it kindly from me either," Şelal shot back. Armesh's only reply was to shrug, an ultimatum, in effect, to which Şelal rolled her eyes. "You have until morning with your precious ring," she said, then stalked away.

Armesh led Leorah and Devorah to their tent, where a guard was posted. They heard Armesh's footsteps receding as the two of them sat in stunned silence. The sun went down, and for much of that time, Leorah sat cross-legged, silently staring at the ring. "I miss them so," she finally said. "Mother. Father. Little Emil."

"I do, too."

Seeming to lose all her energy at once, Leorah lay down. Devorah cradled her as Leorah had done the other night. This time, Leorah was the one holding a ring, though it was not flawed. It was the one that held power, the one that offered hope, if only Devorah could learn its secrets. As Leorah's breathing fell into a slow, smooth rhythm, Devorah's mind was running wild. When she was sure Leorah was asleep, she took the ring from where it was clutched in her hands, then left the tent. The two guards stopped her.

"Am I to be held as well, then?"

"We were told to watch you both," said the larger of the two, the one wearing only sirwal pants and rope sandals.

"She's feeling ill. I'm going to speak with Bagra."

"Tell me what remedies she needs," the guard said. "I'll get them for her."

Summoning every last dram of Leorah's fire, Devorah stepped forward and poked him in the center of his bronzed chest. "My sister is leaving in the morning with a King of Sharakhai. I may never see her again. *I* will get the remedies she needs, not you."

She stalked away before either could respond. One grumbled some sort of reply, but to her great relief, neither tried to stop her. She did go to Bagra then, the tribe's physic.

"Leorah can't sleep," Devorah told her once she'd been roused. "And if I know her, she won't be able to for many days."

Lighting a lamp, Bagra frowned, her deep wrinkles standing out like crags over the landscape of her weathered face. The blue tattoos of sun and stars to either side of her eyes pinched as she squinted at Devorah. "What's happened, girl?"

Devorah stared at her as if she couldn't believe her ears. "My *sister* has been promised to King Sukru!"

Bagra frowned. "Has she?"

"Yes! She leaves in the morning. I would send her

away with something that will help ease her into her new life."

Bagra's frown deepened as she turned to her standing chest of drawers. She took a small glass vial, opened one of the drawers, and used a tiny spoon to scoop a small amount of grey powder into it. She held it out to Devorah. "Mix it with hot water, then drink it quick."

"I need more. Enough for a week at least."

"I daresay Sukru has a physic of his own, girl!"

"Enough for two days, then. They may not have the same remedies as you."

Bagra huffed, making her lips flap, a thing that seemed to define her more than anything else. She was the most aggressively taciturn woman Devorah had ever met. Strange for a physic.

"Two nights," Devorah repeated. "It will do my heart good to know she has something from you."

The glare on Bagra's face deepened. Without another word, she scooped more of the powder into the vial, stoppered it, then handed it to Devorah. "Go on, now," she said, then blew out the lamp before Devorah had even exited the tent.

Outside, Devorah tucked the vial away. She was relieved, but the night's most difficult task still lay ahead of her. She headed for the largest of the Rafik tents, the very one she'd visited the other night. "Armesh," she called softly when she arrived at the front flaps. "Armesh, we must speak."

It was Şelal who came to her, however. "Have you not plagued me enough?"

"I must speak with Armesh."

"Go to your tent, Devorah. Better to spend time with your sister in your own tent than waste it in front of mine."

"You don't understand. It was Leorah who sent me."

"What about?"

"She wouldn't say."

"Enough of your games," Şelal said, and made to close the tent, but Devorah stopped her.

"It's to do with my mother. A secret, she said, something she should have told Armesh long ago."

At this Şelal stiffened. "What secret?"

"I told you, she wouldn't tell me, but clearly she wishes to confess it before she's taken to Sharakhai."

Şelal paused, considering. "I will come. She can tell me."

She stepped out, and Devorah began formulating a response, anything to deny her, but just then a scratchy voice came from inside the tent, "Şelal, I will go."

A short while later, Armesh stepped out, rubbing sleep from his eyes. Even in the dim light of the crescent moons, Devorah could see Şelal's discomfort, the way she fidgeted. It seemed clear that she'd recently learned of Armesh's closeness to Devorah and Leorah's mother, Yael.

"I will go," Armesh said before Şelal could object. "She deserves that much."

Şelal's back stiffened, she looked to them both, a dark cloud over her, then swept into the tent without another word.

"Come," Armesh said, and began walking with Devorah toward her tent, where Leorah lay sleeping.

Devorah walked with him only far enough that Şelal would sense nothing amiss, should she be watching, then she tugged on his arm and pointed toward open sand. He seemed unsurprised, and without a word allowed himself to be led away from the cluster of tents.

When they were far enough away, Devorah pulled from the purse at her belt the two amethyst rings. They glittered in the moonlight. "I must know how it works, Armesh."

Armesh reached out unerringly and took the ring that was whole. She thought he would deny her, that he would look upon her sadly, as so many seemed to do, and tell her to return to her tent. To her great surprise, he did not. To her great surprise, he told her all.

"We took it into the desert near sunset," he began, "far away from the tribe, far away from watching eyes. Only then did your mother reveal its secrets to me."

Her mind afire, her movements frenzied, Devorah returned to her tent as the sun began to burn behind the peaks of the eastern mountains. She stoked the coals of the oven, boiled water. After pouring the double dose of the powder into a mug and dousing it with hot water, she roused Leorah and told her she'd gone to Bagra to get a special tea, one that would calm her nerves for the coming day.

"It tastes foul," Leorah said, setting the cup down.

"Drink it," Devorah said. "It will help, I promise."

Leorah seemed doubtful, but she accepted the mug and with a vacant expression sipped at it while Devorah busied herself, preparing the beautiful desert dress Leorah had been working on for weeks, choosing earrings and a necklace and a host of silver bangles Leorah favored when she was feeling fancy. She laid out Leorah's best sandals as well, the strappy ones that came from the endless hills of Kundhun.

"You don't have to dress me," Leorah said dreamily. "I'm not a child."

"Today I will dress you," Devorah replied, adopting the same air their mother always used when she needed them to listen.

Leorah smiled, nodded once, then finished the last of her tea. "I'm tired," she said.

Devorah was starting to feel desperate, knowing what she said now might be the last words she ever spoke to Leorah. She stifled the hopeless thoughts lest Leorah catch on. "There's time yet. I'll make a bit of flatbread and honey, just like you like it, dusted with crushed pistachios, yes?" Even as Leorah's eyes closed, her smile widened. "Go on," Devorah said. "Lie down. I'll wake you."

Leorah did, scrunching her down pillow until she found a comfortable position. It reminded Devorah of when they were young, a memory that knifed through Devorah's heart. "I'm sorry I'm so difficult."

Devorah leaned over and kissed the crown of Leorah's head. "You aren't difficult."

"I am so," she whispered, "and I ruined everything."

"You fight for what you believe in. You fight for yourself, but also for me." When she heard Leorah's breaths deepen, she leaned in and kissed her one last time. "Today, however, *I* will fight for *you*."

Moving with haste, Devorah pulled on Leorah's favorite dress, put on the earrings and necklace, strapped on the sandals. Then she took up the two rings: the dead amethyst and the other, the one that felt alive. The dead one she put on the middle finger of her right hand. Then she retrieved a belly chain, a thing she'd found sexy but had never once worn since buying it at a caravanserai when she was fifteen. She strung the living ring through the chain and then, after hiking up her dress, clasped it around her waist. After maneuvering the ring until it rested at the small of her back, she smoothed the dress back into place. It felt so conspicuous.

Breath of the desert, how will anyone fail to see it?

The only thing that calmed her nerves was the fact that she need fool only one man: a King. If *he* noticed, this would all be over, but that somehow comforted her, gave her focus. It was a thing for her to strive for instead of worrying about Leorah and Şelal and Armesh and all the rest.

Outside the tent, the camp was coming to life. Devorah's hands were shaking. Gripping them tightly, she gave Leorah one last look. Her tears felt hot along her cheeks. She let them flow. It would only add to the effect of a woman distressed.

"See you when you wake," she said, a thing they used to whisper to one another before falling asleep as children.

She left the tent, tying the flaps in terrible knots to dissuade anyone from entering, and made her way with the guards toward the edge of the camp, toward Sukru's galleon. Some few were already up. A few waved. Most merely watched. She ignored them all, trudging stolidly toward the dark galleon, which looked in the morning light like some monstrosity, an ancient desert wyrm, coiled and waiting.

The guards backed away as she neared the ship's long skimwood runners. "I would speak with King Sukru!"

A Blade Maiden arrived at the gunwales. She stared down, her face hidden behind the veil of her turban. "The Kings of Sharakhai are not called upon. The *King* calls upon *you*."

Devorah ignored her. "I would speak with King Sukru!"

"Shout like that again, Biting Shield, and I'll make sure it doesn't happen again."

"I am to be his *wife*!" she railed. "Can I not speak

with my future husband if I wish it?"

In answer, the Blade Maiden seemed to tip over the side of the ship. Head over heels she spun to land just next to Devorah on the sand. Her hand shot out and struck Devorah across one cheek. Devorah reeled, tried to escape, but the Maiden had already grabbed a fistful of hair at the back of Devorah's head. She pulled Devorah close, rasped in her ear. "You are not the King's wife yet. Shout and wake my King, and I'll be tempted to see if he'll forgive me for taking a finger."

"I've come with his ring!" She held up her right hand. The ring glittered in the early morning light. "He wanted it last night!"

"And coward that you were, you sent your shaikh to deny him." Quick as an asp, she snatched Devorah's hand and pulled her curving kenshar from its sheath. Devorah tried to deny her, but the Maiden was too fast, too strong. Soon enough she had Devorah's pinky gripped tight, the kenshar's edge held between it and the next finger, ready to slice it away. "Perhaps I'll keep going until I come to the one with the ring, yes?"

"I only wish to make amends!"

The Maiden seemed not to hear. Her eyes were focused on Devorah's hand, as if she could think of nothing but following through on her threat.

"Enough!" an aged voice called from above. They both looked up to find Sukru standing at the gunwales where the Maiden had been only moments ago. "Bring her to me." Then he was gone, though his voice trailed after. "With all her fingers, if you please."

The Maiden was *not* pleased. She shoved Devorah forward, and kept shoving until they reached the gangplank on the far side of the ship. Up Devorah went until she was standing before Sukru near the gunwales. The camp had heard. More and more strode forward, gathering along the sand, watching this strange spectacle unfold.

"I've come to deliver your ring," Devorah said to Sukru.

"So you said." Sukru, a half-head smaller than Devorah, stared into her eyes with a pitiless expression. "And yet I do not have it."

Devorah made no move to take off the ring. Not yet. "I will give it to you. I ask only that you allow me to remain here with the people I love."

"Now why would I do that?" He seemed perfectly perplexed, a galling act that made Devorah wish she had a knife to hand.

Instead, she held up her right hand so that the amethyst glittered before his eyes. "Because what you really want is this. My sister told me. So take it. Take it and the rest of the prizes and enjoy them in Sharakhai."

Sukru looked her up and down, and for a moment she thought she'd made a terrible misstep. The mention of *sister* seemed to have made him assess her anew. Had he recognized her? Did he know who she really was?

A moment later, he said, "Your sister spoke the truth," and her nerves calmed. "I came here for the ring, but it's been a long while since I've taken a bride. You've proven yourself to be a fine woman, if rough along the edges. Burrs can be filed away, though, can they not? Burnished until they shine, the memories of those once-rough edges vanishing like footprints in the desert."

"I wouldn't know, my Lord King."

Sukru chuckled. "I wouldn't know… Well, you will soon enough."

"No," Devorah said.

She'd never had much hope that he would allow her to leave. He was a man who coveted much, and once he'd set his sights on something would never let it go. What she was more worried about was that he would sense the nature of the ring on her right hand, or worse, the one hidden at the small of her back.

On the sand below, more from all three tribes had

gathered, including Şelal, who watched with anger, and Armesh, who watched with mouth agape, and Kirhan, who walked on crutches, staring intently at Devorah and Sukru as he struggled to understand the strange situation unfolding before him.

Devorah pulled the ring from her finger and held it out for Sukru to take. "Please. Take it and leave me. I'll never love you."

Sukru's face screwed up in a look of pure contempt. "What care have I for *love*?"

Devorah tossed the ring at Sukru's slippered feet. It made a pathetic sound against the deck. "I *will not* marry you."

Sukru bent over and picked up the ring. He seemed entranced by it. "In the eyes of the gods, you are already my bride."

He snapped his fingers. The Maiden immediately made for Devorah, but before she could come close, Devorah lunged for the handle of Sukru's wide-bladed knife at his belt. She drew it from its sheath, a blade so curved it looked like an ox's horn.

"Never!" she screamed.

Only when she was sure the Maiden was on her way to stop her did she slice for the King.

The Blade Maiden barreled across Devorah's path,

one hand gripping the wrist that held the knife. In one powerful move, Devorah was slammed to the deck and the knife was twisted from her grasp. The Maiden held it to Devorah's throat. A line burned across her skin, but not deeply. She wouldn't kill Devorah yet, not without leave from her King.

"Lift her," Sukru said.

The Maiden complied with cruel efficiency, until Devorah was standing awkwardly, eye-to-eye with the King.

Sukru flicked his fingers. "The knife."

The Maiden handed it over.

Sukru handled it easily, a collector of rare artifacts examining some new treasure. "Never, you say?"

"One day you'll not be able to keep that knife from my hands, or another just like it."

"You would die before coming to Sharakhai—a land of riches, a place of infinite sounds and smells and tastes, a place of wonders—all because you fear you cannot love me?" He no longer seemed angry, only curious.

Devorah's response was to spit into his face.

The crowd on the sand gasped.

The Maiden wrenched Devorah's arm so hard Devorah screamed.

Sukru wiped the spittle from his face, but then motioned the Maiden for calm. He took a step closer. Gripped the knife. "So be it."

And drove it deep into her gut.

The voice of the crowd lifted in shock, some shouting, "No!"

Pain blossomed, and Devorah wondered, knowing they thought her to be Leorah, *Would they react so for me?* And immediately after, *What does it matter, you foolish girl?*

She felt herself being lifted. Felt the sky open up before her as the world became weightless, floating. She fell hard against the sand. Saw it lift in a cloud around her, a pall of spindrift with a sound like falling rain.

"No one will touch her!"

Sukru's voice, yet Kirhan still came. He dropped to her side, pain momentarily masking the worry in his eyes.

Have you been hurt? she tried to say to him, but the words wouldn't come.

Her mind drifted from Kirhan to Armesh, to their conversation last night. "Your mother and I used the amethyst once." He had stared into its facets, enchanted, perhaps remembering that day. "We were in love, then. Or as in love as children can be. Near dusk we trekked far into the desert, to a small oasis with a cave beside it. We built a fire, and that night, as the sun was setting, she put the ring on. She asked that I close my eyes, that I feel for its pull. I didn't know what she meant. I kept staring until she leaned forward and kissed me, then brushed one hand over my eyes. Keep them closed, she told me. *Feel* for it.

"I did, and soon understood what she meant. The stone was a well. A place of infinite depth. Good, she said, then asked that I step into it." Armesh had paused then, blinking as he stared at the ring. Tears welled in his eyes. "I was scared, but I did as she asked. It was simple once I found it. I stepped into that new place, and so did she. While the sun set, we shared with one another—me in her form, her in mine. We walked around the oasis, admired the beauty of the desert while holding hands, caught in the spell of the amethyst."

He'd wiped his tears and held out the ring for Devorah to take. "Feel for that well, Devorah, and you'll find it. Let me tell Leorah the rest."

Devorah had taken the ring. "If you loved my mother so, why did you never fight for her?"

Armesh smiled. "I would never have admitted it then, but she was too bright a star for one such as me.

I never stopped loving her, and I think she loved me in her own way, but in the end, the fates found her the right man." Devorah was crying, too. He wiped her tears away. "I still have that one night to treasure. I will *always* have it. But now, far beyond the imaginings of my youth, here you are, Leorah as well, a pair of perfect jewels made from her, much like these very stones."

"Leorah is hardly perfect"—Devorah had laughed—"and the gods know very well that *I'm* not."

Armesh had smiled wryly. "Nearly perfect, then."

Laying there on the sand, staring up into Kirhan's face, Devorah did as Armesh had instructed. She closed her eyes to the morning sky. She reached for the amethyst.

She'd hardly begun when she felt it. Just as Armesh had said, a great pool of violet now stood before her. How had she never noticed it before? It seemed impossible, but there it was. Waiting for her. Beckoning.

And so she went. She stepped inside.

And the world around her faded.

Near nightfall, Leorah stood before a freshly made grave—a deep pit in the sand, now open to the sky. Devorah lay within, wearing *her* favorite dress, the one made from a supple cloth dyed persimmon and lemon with finely embroidered cuffs and collar. Her hair had been braided. Her skin had been cleaned of the blood.

So much blood.

She looked neither peaceful nor in pain. Rather, she looked as though she'd forgotten the world and had no further use for it.

Devorah's rites were spoken to the assembled, a massive crowd made up of all three tribes. Several had spoken in her memory. Şelal had asked to join them, and Leorah had granted it. The shaikh of Tribe Rafik had shared eloquent words. Touching. She'd known more about Devorah than Leorah had ever guessed. Armesh spoke as well, more touching words, though Leorah hardly heard them.

Soon it was done. Many near the edges, never having known Devorah, left. Those nearer picked up fistfuls of sand. When they came near, they allowed the sand to drop in a stream into the grave while whispering to the gods, hopes and prayers for Devorah's life in the farther fields. When they were done, many stood at the ready, waiting for Leorah to do the same.

Leorah shook her head, her hands clasped tightly

before her. She couldn't do it. She wouldn't. It wouldn't be right. They stared at her, confused, until Şelal motioned them to continue, at which point they filled in the hole. When the grave looked indistinguishable from the rest of the landscape, Şelal ushered the crowd away.

Only two remained. Armesh and Kirhan.

Armesh looked awkwardly between Kirhan and Leorah, looking as though he wanted to say more but couldn't, or wouldn't, with Kirhan near. "You'll let me know if you need me."

Leorah nodded numbly. "Of course."

She couldn't decide if she was angry with him or not. He'd been involved. He'd held Devorah's hand as she'd walked toward her fate. But who owned more of the blame than Leorah herself? How could Armesh be faulted when Leorah had blinded herself to the dangers?

Armesh embraced her, then followed the rest, leaving Leorah alone with Kirhan, who'd defied his King to remain here in the desert. Leorah was confused about his presence. She wasn't yet sure if she was happy to have him here or not.

"Why didn't you go?" she asked him.

"I would never have forgiven myself if I'd left."

"But Sukru threatened you. He threatened your family, in front of *everyone*. They told me."

He seemed embarrassed by the words. "One cannot live under the yoke of fear forever. And I would not leave before…"

"Before what?"

"Before we'd spoken." He looked strangely shy, this man, this champion.

They stood near the edge of the desert, where the sand gave way to the slopes of the mountains. Around them, small insects buzzed, some caught in the light of the lowering sun. "I'm glad you stayed," she said at last. "Soon we'll have our talk, but not now. Not here."

The sun lit half of Kirhan's handsome face in a ruddy glow. The other was left in shadow, like a man standing between two worlds. *Precisely what he is now.*

Kirhan nodded, clasped his hands to his forehead, a sign of peace, then left her to her thoughts.

Still gripping her right hand tight, Leorah strode away from the camp, away from the sand, and took to the hard-packed earth below the mountains. She trekked up toward a rocky ledge, then sat down as the sun neared the horizon.

Only then did she open her right hand to reveal the ring and the amethyst set within it. From the moment she'd accepted it from Armesh, she'd felt something. She'd felt it throughout the day. She'd felt it throughout the burial. She felt it now, stronger than ever.

Leorah fumbled for words, unsure where to begin. The anger over what her sister had done bubbled up inside her, as did the relief and gratitude over being saved from marrying Sukru, of being whisked away to Sharakhai like Tulathan to Yerinde's tower.

"Do you suppose he's angry?" Leorah finally asked while staring at the setting sun.

Like a new moon rising, Devorah's presence grew, crystallizing into something beautiful inside her. "Over losing his bride or his prize?" Devorah's words drifted to her like seeds on the wind.

"He never cared for me. I was always a beast meant to deliver him our ring. Or at best a thing to lust over."

"He'll suspect by now the ring he has is useless," Devorah said. "I imagine he's *very* angry."

"It might force his return."

"No. That would be like admitting defeat. He can't be certain about the nature of the ring yet. He'll return to Sharakhai and consult with the other Kings. He'll call wise women and men to him. In the end, he'll find nothing. He'll rail. But then his attention will move on to other, brighter things. It is the way of the Kings of Sharakhai."

Leorah didn't want to talk about Kings any longer.

"I don't know how to feel!" she confessed to the cooling desert sky.

"How to feel?" Devorah replied. Her voice was ephemeral, but it grew stronger with each passing moment. "Feel all of it. The sorrow and the joy. The anger and loneliness. The same as me."

"But we're not the same. You're trapped while I'm yet free."

"I knew the way of things when I went to Sukru's ship."

"But it doesn't have to be so," Leorah said, readying the secret, the hope she'd harbored across the day.

She could sense Devorah's confusion. "What do you mean?"

"The stone. It holds your soul, but it can just as easily hold mine." Leorah spread her arms wide. She touched her own cheeks. "We can trade places, you and I. We can share in this, the poorest of our forms!"

"Leorah—"

"The stone is particular in its magic. We can only do so at dawn and dusk, but what matter is that! You may have the day if you like. Or the night. You've always loved the moon and stars. Now it shall be yours!"

"Leorah—"

"In truth," Leorah went on, "this is a gift. I've never known you as well as I might have. As well as I should. Do not think to hide away in a stone. *Share* with me, sister. Share with me, and live!"

Leorah felt tears slipping down her cheeks. She wasn't sure if they were Devorah's or her own.

"Both," Devorah said.

With that, Leorah felt her acceptance.

They spoke for a time as the sun went down. They laughed. They cried. And slowly, Leorah felt herself being swallowed, felt her bodily self go numb. When the light from the sun began to fade, it was no longer Leorah who stretched out her arms and legs, nor she who gripped her fingers, nor scrunched her toes. Leorah *felt* these things, but they were distant as memories. They contented her, however. They were like the strokes of her mother's hand, an embrace in her father's arms.

As Leorah's sense of her own body failed entirely, Devorah stood.

"Thank you, sister," she said, and headed toward the glittering camp.

Continue the adventure in *Twelve Kings in Sharakhai*. A sample of the book's first chapter follows...

Chapter 1

In a small room beneath the largest of Sharakhai's fighting pits, Çeda sat on a wooden bench, tightening her fingerless gloves. The room was cool, even chill compared to the ever-present heat of the city. Painted ceramic tiles lined the walls. A mismatched jumble of wooden benches and shelves that had clearly seen decades of abuse made it feel well loved if not well cared for. Were Çeda any other dirt dog, she would have sat in one of the rooms on the far side of the pits, the ones that hosted dozens of men and women. But Çeda was given special dispensation, and had been since winning her first bout at the age of fourteen.

By the gods, five years already.

She tightened her hands into fists, enjoying the creak of the leather, the feel of the chain mail wrapped around the backs of her hands and knuckles. She checked the straps of her armor. Her greaves, her bracers, her heavy battle skirt. And finally her breastplate. All of them had once been dyed white—the color of a wolf's bared teeth—but now the armor was so well used that much of the leather's natural brown shone through. *Well and good*, Çeda thought. It felt used. Lived in. Kissed by battle. Exactly the way she liked it.

She picked up her bright steel helm and set it on her lap. She stared into the iron mask fixed across the front—a mask of a woman's face, cold and expressionless in the face of battle. Affixed to the top of the helm was a wolf's pelt, teeth bared, muzzle resting along the crown.

Echoing down the corridor came a voice that sounded old and hoary, a mountain come to life. "They're ready." It was Pelam.

Çeda glanced toward the arched doorway with the blood-red curtains strung across it. "Coming," she said, then returned her attention to the helm. She ran her fingers over the many nicks in the metal, over the mask's empty eyes—

Tulathan grant me foresight.

—stroked the rough fur of the wolf's pelt—

Thaash guide my sword.

—then pulled the helm over her braided black hair and strapped it tightly on.

As the weight of the armor settled over her, she parted the heavy curtains and hiked up the sloping tunnel into the heat of the noontime sun. The walls of the fighting pit towered around her, and above them, arranged in concentric circles, were the seats of the stadium. *It's going to be a good day for Osman.* Already there were several hundred waiting for the bout to begin.

Roughly half the spectators called the city of Sharakhai home; they knew the pits inside and out, knew the regular dirt dogs as well. The other half were visitors to the desert's amber jewel. They'd come to trade or find fortune in a city that offered greater opportunities than they'd had back home. It rankled that so many came here, to Çeda's home, and lived off it like fleas on a dog. Though she could hardly complain—

A boy in a teal kaftan pointed to Çeda wildly and called, "The White Wolf! The Wolf has come to fight!" and the crowd rose to their feet as one, craning their necks to see.

—the pits paid well enough.

A ragged cheer went up as she strode to the center of the pit and joined the circle of eleven other fighters. The money men in the stands began calling out odds for the White Wolf. She hadn't even been chosen to fight yet, so no one would know who her opponent would be, but many still flocked to be the first to wager their coin on her.

The other dirt dogs watched Çeda warily. Some knew her, but just like those in the audience, many of these fighters had come from distant kingdoms to try their hand against the best fighters in Sharakhai. Three women stood among those gathered—two well muscled, the third an absolute brute; she outweighed Çeda by three stone at least. The rest were men, some brawny, others lithe. One, however, was a tower of a man wearing a beaten leather breastplate and a conical helm with chain mail that lapped against his broad shoulders. Haluk. He stood a full head and a half taller than Çeda and stared at her like an ox readying a charge.

In response, Çeda strode toward him and pressed her thumb to an exposed edge on the back of her mailed gloves. She pressed hard enough to pierce skin, to draw blood. Haluk stared at her with confusion, then a wicked sort of glee, as Çeda stopped in front of him and pressed her bloody thumb to the center of his leather breastplate.

The crowd roared.

A new flurry of betting rose, while the rest of the audience jockeyed for position against the rim of the pit.

Çeda had just marked Haluk for her own, an ancient gesture that not all dirt dogs would respect, but these would, she reckoned. None of them would wish to fight Haluk, not in their first bout of the day. When Çeda turned away and returned to her place in the circle, all but ignoring Haluk, the naked anger on his face was slowly replaced with a look of cool assessment. *Good,* Çeda thought. He'd taken the bait and would surely choose her if she didn't choose him first.

When some but not all of the betting flurry had died down, Pelam stepped out from another darkened tunnel. The calls of betting rose to a tumult as the audience saw the first bout was ready to begin.

Pelam wore a jeweled vest, a brown kufi, and a red kaftan that was not only fashionable but fine, save for its hem, which was hopelessly dusty from its days sweeping the pit floors. In one of Pelam's skeletal hands he held a woven basket. As the fighters parted for him, he stepped to the rough center of their circle and flipped the basket lid open. After one last check around him to ensure all was ready, he shot his hand into basket's confines and lifted a horned viper as long as his lanky legs. The snake wriggled, swelling its hood and hissing, baring its fangs for all to see.

Pelam knew his business, but the snake made Çeda's hackles rise. Bites were rare but not unheard of, especially if one of the fighters was inexperienced and jumped when the snake drew near. Çeda knew enough to remain still, but foreigners didn't always follow Pelam's careful pre-bout instructions, and it wasn't always the person who jumped that the snakes chose to sink their fangs into.

As Pelam held the writhing snake, each of the fighters spread their legs wide until their sandaled or booted feet butted up against each other's. After a glance at each of the fighter's stances, and finding them proper, Pelam dropped the snake and stepped away.

It lay there, coiling itself tightly. The crowd shouted to the baked desert air, their voices rising to a fever pitch as each yelled the name of their chosen fighter. The fighters themselves remained silent. Oddly, the snake slithered toward Pelam for a moment, then seemed to think better of it and turned to glide over the sand to Çeda's left, then turned once more. And slithered straight through Haluk's legs.

Silence followed as a pit boy ran and snatched the viper by its tail, lowering it back into its basket as the snake spun like a woodworker's auger.

Pelam calmly awaited Haluk's choice.

The big man didn't hesitate. He made straight for Çeda and spat on the ground at her feet.

The crowd went wild. "The Oak of the Guard has chosen the White Wolf!"

Oak indeed. Haluk was a captain of the Silver Spears, and a tree of a man, but he was also a particularly *cruel* man, and it was time he learned a lesson.

Like jackals to a kill, the news drew spectators from neighboring pits. The stands were soon brimming with them.

As the rest of the fighters exited the pit, a dozen boys jogged out from the tunnels bearing wooden swords and shields and clubs. Çeda, as the challenged, would normally be allowed to choose weapons first, but she followed ancient custom; she had marked him, and thus *she* was the true challenger, not Haluk, so she bowed her head and waved to the weapons, granting first choice to Haluk. Most would have returned the honor, but Haluk merely grunted and chose one of the few weapons meant for both him and his opponent: the fetters.

The noise of the crowd rose until it was akin to thunder. Some laughed, others clapped. Some few even stared with naked worry at Çeda, who had clearly just been put at a severe disadvantage by Haluk's choice of weapon.

The fetters was a length of tough, braided leather. It was wrapped tightly around one of each fighter's wrists, keeping them in close proximity and ensuring a brawl.

While glaring intently at Haluk, Çeda held out her left hand, allowing Pelam to slip the end of the fetters around her wrist and tighten it. Pelam did the same to Haluk, then took a small brass gong and mallet from one of the boys.

The pit was cleared so that only Çeda, Haluk, and Pelam remained.

The doors to the tunnels closed.

And then, after a dramatic pause in which Pelam held the gong chest-high between the two fighters, he struck it and stepped away.

There was slack in the fetters, a situation Haluk would quickly attempt to remedy—his best hope, after all, lay in controlling Çeda's movement—but Çeda was ready for it. The moment Haluk lunged in to grab as much of the leather rope as he could, she darted forward, leaping and snapping a kick at his chin. When he retreated, Çeda charged, a move he clearly hadn't been expecting. His eyes widened as Çeda grabbed his clumsily raised arm and sent her fist crashing into his cheek.

She could feel the chain mail dig deep into the fighting gloves she wore, but it was worse for Haluk. He fell unceremoniously onto his rump, his conical helm flying off and thumping onto the dry dirt, kicking up dust as it went.

The crowd stood and howled its delight.

As his helm skidded well out of reach, Haluk rolled backward over his shoulder and came to a stand, so quickly that Çeda had no time to rush forward and end it.

Haluk raised one hand to his cheek, felt the blood from the patterned cuts the mail had left in his skin, then stared at his own hand with a look like he'd disappointed himself. And then his eyes went hard. He'd been pure bluster before, trying to intimidate Çeda, but now he was seething mad.

None so blind as a wrathful man, Çeda thought.

Haluk crouched warily and began wrapping the

fetters around his left wrist, over and over, slowly taking up the slack. Çeda retreated and pulled hard on the fetters, putting her entire body into it, making the leather scrape painfully along Haluk's arm. He ignored it and continued to wrap the restraints around his wrist. Çeda yanked on the fetters again, but he blunted the tactic with well-timed grips on the leather, the muscles along his arm rippling and bulging. He grinned, showing two rows of ragged teeth.

Çeda sent several kicks toward his thighs and knees, attacks meant more to test Haluk's reflexes than anything else. Haluk blocked them easily. She was just about to yank on the fetters again when he loosened his grip and rushed her. Çeda stumbled, pretending to lose her balance, and when Haluk came close she dove to her right and swept a leg across his ankles.

He fell in a heap, the breath whooshing from his lungs.

He grabbed for Çeda and managed to snag her ankle, but one swift kick from Çeda's free heel and she was up and dancing away while Haluk rose slowly to his feet.

The crowd howled again, many of the foreigners joining in, though they had no idea why. The Sharakani knew, though. They understood why bouts like this were so very rare.

Haluk hadn't been defeated in more than ten years of fighting in the pits. Çeda had rarely lost since her first bout, and she'd lost none in the past three years. Everyone knew how widely the story of this bout would be told, especially if Çeda took him in so cleanly a fashion. Few would dare utter the tale within Haluk's hearing, but the entire city would be alive with it by the end of the day.

And Haluk knew it. He stared into Çeda's eyes with an intensity that reeked of desperation. He would not be so easy to take again.

As the two of them squared off once more, the crowd went completely and eerily silent. The only sound was of Haluk's ragged breathing and Çeda's strong but controlled breaths from within the confines of her helm.

Haluk took one tentative step forward. Çeda stepped away, snatching up some of the slack in the fetters as she went. Haluk did the same until they both held a quarter of the length in reserve, leaving them a scant few strides from one another.

Haluk took two measured steps toward her. He was trying to close the distance, but he was no longer reckless. He was cautious, as a man who'd become a captain of Sharakhai's guard *should* be.

Çeda kicked at his legs again, connecting but doing little damage. That wasn't the point, though. She had to keep him on his guard until she was ready to move in. She snapped another kick and retreated, but she could only go so far. Haluk had drawn up more of the fetters, so Çeda released some of hers. Haluk strode forward, taking up more of the braided rope. Which forced Çeda to release more. Until she had none left.

He drew sharply on it, keeping his center low, his balance steady, and Çeda was drawn forward until she was just out of his striking range.

The crowd began to stamp their feet, the sound of it reverberating in the pit, but otherwise they were silent, rapt.

Haluk pulled again, harder now that they were so close. And that's when Çeda moved.

Using the tension on the fetters to pull herself forward, she launched herself with a leap, straight into his body. In his surprise, Haluk grasped for her neck, but she slipped her forearms inside his and grabbed two fistfuls of his lanky brown hair. She wrapped her legs around his waist, twisted them around his thighs, and locked her feet around his knees, hoping to trip him up and end this once and for all.

He didn't fall, however. He was too big. Too strong. And he did exactly what she would have done. He rose up, preparing to slam her against the ground.

At the high point of his lift, she did the only thing she could: she clung hard to his neck and waist.

When they came down, they came down hard. Pain burst across Çeda's back and rump as Haluk's full weight bore down on her. Through her coughing and the ringing in her ears, she could hear him laughing. "Foolish move, girl."

He tried to lift away, but she'd locked her arms around his neck. Her legs hugged tightly to his waist. He was strong, but he had no leverage to break her grip. Again and again he tried to lift himself away from her to give himself room to punch, but each time he did, she began slipping her arms around his neck to cut off his blood. He would drop to prevent it, and then they were back, body to body, breath coming hard and fast, the very intimate duel continuing as each struggled for any small amount of leverage.

Once, when he lifted his head too far away, she crashed her forehead against his. The lip of her helm left a long cut against his skin. Blood seeped down his forehead, along his nose. It pattered against her steel mask, filling her nostrils with the smell of it.

Then, in a sudden and furious move, Haluk lifted, slipping a forearm across her throat, managing to pin her down.

Immediately the crowd was up, shouting, raging. But it all became little more than a keen ringing in Çeda's ears. She heard her own heart thrumming. Felt Haluk's arm tighten further.

It was a strong move, a *wise* move under the conditions, but he'd left himself open. She slipped her right hand down along his left arm, near his elbow, where she'd have the most leverage, and pushed. She let out a guttural cry while muscling his arm up, which had the effect of propelling herself down along his body, just enough to slip her head under his armpit and out of the lock.

He tried to slip his arm back under her neck, but before he could, she grabbed the buckles along the far edge of his breastplate and hauled herself away, and now she was halfway to his back. Exactly where she wanted to be.

She reached her left arm—the one tied to the fetters—up and over his head. The rope slipped neatly down along his face and across his neck. Immediately she tightened her grip and drew the fetters back.

Haluk knew what was happening—he tried to

throw her off, at least enough to get his fingers beneath the fetters—but her grip was too sure. Still, he was a bull of a man. She grunted while gritting her teeth and arching her back. Her arms strained like cording on a ship's sails.

She thought surely he would have pounded his hand against the ground by now, giving up the match, or fallen unconscious, but he hadn't. He still struggled for air, his breath coming out in a desperate hiss, his mouth frothing from it. And then finally, all at once, his body went slack.

Çeda didn't hear the strike of Pelam's gong, marking the end of the bout.

But the crowd she heard.

Their elation could no longer be contained. They stomped their feet. They shook their fists. "The Wolf has won! The Wolf has won!"

Ignoring them, Çeda pushed Haluk onto his back and straddled his chest. She unwrapped the fetters and saw the blood drain from him, casting his face in a strange, deathly pallor.

His eyes blinked open. He stared into Çeda's eyes with a look of confusion, then took in his surroundings as if he had no idea where he was. The roaring crowd and Çeda's masked face soon registered, though, and a look of deep and inexpressible anger stole over him.

Çeda leaned down until they were chest-to-chest and whispered into his ear. "The next time you take your hands to your daughter, Haluk Emet'ava"—she pressed the thumbnail of her right hand into his side, in the depression between his fourth and fifth ribs—"it will go much worse for you." She leaned closer still and whispered, "The next time, it will be a knife in the dark, not a beating in the light." She rose, her legs still straddling him, and stared down into his eyes. "Do you understand?"

Haluk blinked. He made no acknowledgement of her demand, but there was shame in his eyes, a shame that spoke the truth of his crimes better than words ever could.

Like a wedge driving ever further into a thick piece of wood, she pressed her thumb deeper. "I would hear your answer."

He grimaced against the discomfort, licked his lips and glanced to the cheering crowd. Then he nodded to her. "I understand."

Çeda nodded back, then stood and stepped away.

Pelam had watched this exchange with a glint in his eye that landed somewhere between curious and concerned, but he made no mention of it. He merely turned and presented Çeda to the crowd with a bow of his head and a flourish of his hand. As some howled and others collected their winnings, Çeda was surprised to see that Osman himself had come to watch—Osman, the owner of these pits, a retired pit fighter himself, the man she'd had to trick to earn her first bout.

How far we've come since then.

He stood with the crowd on the topmost row. He was one of the very few—along with Pelam—who knew her true identity. She had no idea how long he'd been watching, but surely he'd caught the end. She couldn't tell if he was pleased or not. Çeda gave an exaggerated nod to the crowd, but she and Osman both knew it was meant for him.

He nodded back, then tugged his ear, which meant he wished to speak.

To speak, and perhaps more.

***Twelve Kings in Sharakhai* is available wherever fine books are sold.**

Twelve Kings in Sharakhai is the exciting new Arabian Nights-inspired epic fantasy from the critically acclaimed author of The Lays of Anuskaya.

Sharakhai, the great city of the desert, center of commerce and culture, has been ruled from time immemorial by twelve kings—cruel, ruthless, powerful, and immortal. With their army of Silver Spears, their elite company of Blade Maidens, and their holy defenders, the terrifying asirim, the Kings uphold their positions as undisputed, invincible lords of the desert. There is no hope of freedom for any under their rule.

Or so it seems, until Çeda, a brave young woman from the west end slums, defies the Kings' laws by going outside on the holy night of Beht Zha'ir. What she learns that night sets her on a path that winds through both the terrible truths of the Kings' mysterious history and the hidden riddles of her own heritage. Together, these secrets could finally break the iron grip of the Kings' power…if the nigh-omnipotent Kings don't find her first.

With Blood Upon the Sand, Book Two of The Song of the Shattered Sands...

Çeda, now a Blade Maiden in service to the kings of Sharakhai, trains as one of their elite warriors, gleaning secrets even as they send her on covert missions to further their rule. She knows the dark history of the asirim—that hundreds of years ago they were enslaved to the kings against their will—but when she bonds with them as a Maiden, chaining them to her, she feels their pain as if her own. They hunger for release, they demand it, but with the power of the gods compelling them, they find the yokes around their necks unbreakable.

When Çeda and Emre are drawn into a plot of the blood mage, Hamzakiir, they sail across the desert to learn the truth, and a devastating secret is revealed, one that may very well shatter the power of the hated kings. They plot quickly to take advantage of it, but it may all be undone if Çeda cannot learn to navigate the shifting tides of power in Sharakhai and control the growing anger of the asirim that threatens to overwhelm her.

A Veil of Spears, Book Three of The Song of the Shattered Sands...

The Night of Endless Swords was a bloody battle that saw the death of one of Sharakhai's immortal kings. When former pit fighter Çeda narrowly escapes the battle and flees into the desert, she takes with her the secrets she learned while posing as a Blade Maiden. Foremost among these is the revelation that the asirim, the kings' frightening immortal slaves, are in fact Çeda's own ancestors, survivors of the fabled thirteenth tribe.

Çeda returns to Sharakhai, hoping to break the chains of the enslaved asirim and save her people. She soon discovers that the once-unified front of the kings is crumbling. Feeling their power slipping away, the kings vie for control over the city and the desert beyond.

As Çeda works to free the asirim and rally them to the defense of the thirteenth tribe, the Kings of Sharakhai prepare for a grand clash that may decide the fate of all.

Of Sand and Malice Made, a Shattered Sands novel...

Çeda is the youngest pit fighter in the history of Sharakhai. She's made her name in the arena as the fearsome White Wolf. None but her closest friends and allies know her true identity. But this all changes when she crosses the path of Rümayesh, an ehrekh, a sadistic creature forged aeons ago by the god of chaos.

The ehrekh are desert dwellers, but for centuries Rümayesh has lurked in the dark corners of Sharakhai, combing the populace for jewels that might interest her. Çeda flees the ehrekh's attentions, but that only makes Rümayesh covet her even more. Rümayesh grows violent. She threatens to unmask Çeda as the White Wolf, but the danger grows infinitely worse when she turns her attention to Çeda's friends. Çeda is horrified. She's seen firsthand the suffering left in Rümayesh's wake.

As Çeda fights to protect the people dearest to her, Rümayesh comes closer to attaining her prize and the struggle becomes a battle for Çeda's very soul.

The critically acclaimed trilogy, The Lays of Anuskaya, is now available in an omnibus edition.

Among inhospitable and unforgiving seas stands Khalakovo, a mountainous archipelago of seven islands, its prominent eyrie stretching a thousand feet into the sky. Serviced by windships bearing goods and dignitaries, Khalakovo's eyrie stands at the crossroads of world trade. But all is not well in Khalakovo. Conflict has erupted between the ruling Landed, the indigenous Aramahn, and the fanatical Maharraht, and a wasting disease has grown rampant over the past decade. Now, Khalakovo is to play host to the Nine Dukes, a meeting which will weigh heavily upon Khalakovo's future.

When an elemental spirit attacks an incoming windship, Prince Nikandr, is tasked with finding the child prodigy believed to be behind the summoning. Can the Dukes, thirsty for revenge, be held at bay?

Can Khalakovo be saved? The elusive answer drifts upon the Winds of Khalakovo…

Find more adventures in other worlds with *Lest Our Passage Be Forgotten & Other Stories*…

With *The Winds of Khalakovo*, Bradley P. Beaulieu established himself as a talented new voice in epic fantasy. Now, with the release of his premiere short story collection, Beaulieu demonstrates his ability to weave tales that explore other worlds in ways that are at once bold, imaginative, and touching. *Lest Our Passage Be Forgotten & Other Stories* contains 17 stories that range from the epic to the heroic, some in print for the first time.

This story collection features two stories from the world of The Lays of Anuskaya. "To the Towers of Tulandan" is a prequel story that tells of Nasim's travels with Ashan before he met Nikandr Khalakovo. And "Prima" is a sequel that reveals what becomes of the three sisters of Vostroma. Also included in the collection is a never-before-published story from Beaulieu's Norse-inspired world of Bryndlholt.

Twelve Kings in Sharakhai marked the start of a bold new epic fantasy series for critically acclaimed author Bradley P. Beaulieu.

In the Stars I'll Find You & Other Tales of Futures Fantastic features Beaulieu's science fictional work, from exploring far-flung worlds to finding what it means to be human through artificial intelligence to the cost of dividing ourselves—or ourself—through the use of technology.

In this short story collection, you'll find eleven tales that explore our very human relationship with technology, some in print for the first time.

About the Author

Bradley P. Beaulieu fell in love with fantasy from the moment he started reading *The Hobbit* in third grade. From that point on, though he tried reading many other things, fantasy became his touchstone. He always came back to it, and when he started to dabble in writing, fantasy—epic fantasy especially—was the type of story he most dearly wished to share.

Twelve Kings in Sharakhai, the first book in his latest series, The Song of the Shattered Sands, was named to over twenty "Best of the Year" lists when it was released in 2015. His critically acclaimed series, The Lays of Anuskaya, has recently been released in omnibus form.

Brad, who recently became a full-time writer, lives in Racine, Wisconsin with his wife and two children. Beyond writing, cooking has become an obsession. His favorite dishes are French, Italian, and Mexican/Southwestern, but he is also fascinated by the art of bread baking.

For more, please visit www.quillings.com.

Made in United States
Orlando, FL
12 February 2024

43618343R00102